Caribbean Prose

An Anthology for Secondary Schools

D1213431

Caribbean Prose

An Anthology for Secondary Schools

edited by Andrew Salkey

Evans

Evans Brothers Limited

Published by Evans Brothers Limited, Montague
House, Russell Square, London, WC1B 5BX

This selection, introduction and notes
© Andrew Salkey 1967
First published 1967
Second impression 1973

Set in 12 on 13 point Granjon
and printed in Great Britain by
Fletcher & Son Ltd, Norwich

PR3270

ISBN 0 237 49692

Contents

For Eliot and Jason

Introduction

I and my teachers and, indeed, their teachers grew up with Charles Kingsley's *Westward Ho!*, Laurence Sterne's *Tristram Shandy,* Charles Reade's *The Cloister and the Hearth,* George Eliot's *Silas Marner* and Jane Austen's *Pride and Prejudice,* to recall only five of the many interesting books in the mainstream of native English literature which were made available for approved reading in the schools' syllabuses throughout the West Indies. My contemporaries and I read these stories under severe pressure both at school and at home, where we were made to feel that every self-respecting student had to read them in order to be *truly* educated. Nevertheless I will long remember the days I spent with Robinson Crusoe, David Copperfield and the others. They were some of the most unforgettable characters I had ever met, and have met up till now.

Today, those at school in the West Indies can still grow up with the usual exposure to the English classics, but with the additional advantage of being able to study and criticize the essentially relevant work of a handful of distinguished West Indian writers. The present anthology, which has been compiled mainly for readers in the fourteen to seventeen age-range, is intended as an introduction to the versatility and remarkable attractiveness of some of these writers – five of them from Jamaica, four from Trinidad, and two each from Guyana and Barbados – in the exacting and sophisticated form of the short story.

I think it is fair to say that this selection has been by far the most difficult I have had to make in my career as an editor of West Indian writing. I have previously edited two adult anthologies of stories but this selection has proved the sternest test of my judgment, taste and all-round ability as an editor. The main reason for my editorial difficulty has been the general unsuitability of most of the existing work of West Indian authors for use in schools. For the most part the novelists have been writing for their adult readers; they have often employed difficult themes and have written in a wide variety of styles. My job has been to 'mine' a few suitable, representative nuggets from a sprawling El Dorado. I have done so with the appropriate trepidation and self-doubt of most editors in my position, bearing in mind throughout that the cardinal sin of any editor is to choose *down* to his readers, rather than to select at a lively and intelligent level.

Before starting work on this collection I did what I imagine most commissioned anthologists do: I asked myself 'What single common factor is it that shapes all short stories?' and the short answer was: the writer's ability to highlight characterization, human behaviour, or a small event, often an ordinary, everyday one, in such a way as to bring it alive for the reader as an immediately recognizable, meaningful entity. With that common factor in mind I have chosen as many different types of short story as I could find, some of them already written in that form, others embedded in novels. I have included examples of the 'slice of life' incident of suspense, adventure, mystery, humour, irony and satire; and there is even a dash of sentimentality in at least two of them.

This wide range of material should also serve another purpose. It will, I hope, depict something of the remarkable diversity of the West Indian way of life, one which not only West Indian readers will easily recognize but which will also be recognized the world over; for, in a very real sense, the West Indies *is* a microcosm: there is its preoccupation with attaining economic well-being and the deep involvement with religion; its continuing attempts to maintain self-respect and individuality in the face of poverty and the crippling lack of opportunity, together with the threat and frightening repercussions of over-population; and again, there is the problem of growing up in a world overshadowed by the threat of a nuclear war; the need simply to cope with man's never-ending struggle with nature and with the terrible effects of personal and public failure.

Some of the more significant books written by West Indians on these and other themes which the reader may come across are C. L. R. James's *Minty Alley, The Black Jacobins* and *Beyond a Boundary;* V. S. Reid's *New Day* and *The Leopard;* George Lamming's *In the Castle of my Skin;* V. S. Naipaul's *A House for Mr Biswas;* John Hearne's *Voices under the Window,* and many of his uncollected short stories in anthologies and magazines published abroad and sold in the West Indies; Roger Mais's *Black Lightning,* a few of his short stories which he brought out privately in Jamaica and some of his journalistic essays; Samuel Selvon's *A Brighter Sun* and very nearly all of his short stories in at least one published collection, in two anthologies of West Indian stories and in most of the back copies of *Bim.* (*Bim* is the excellent Barbadian literary review edited by Frank Collymore: it has been for over twenty years a constant source of encouragement for unpublished West Indian writers and the springboard for quite a number of the well-known published novelists whose early work, mainly short stories, first appeared in its pages).

Then there is Edgar Mittelholzer's *A Morning at the Office* and, for the older reader, *The Life and Death of Sylvia* and the *Kaywana* trilogy: and, of course, Jan Carew's *Black Midas* and *The Wild Coast,* and some of his adventure tales set in the jungles and rain forests of Guyana and published in anthologies and West Indian magazines. I hope, too, that the reader will, when he is about to tackle the specially recommended novels by Edgar Mittelholzer as part of his later reading, accept my recommendation and read Roger Mais's *The Hills Were Joyful Together* and *Brother Man,* together with Neville Dawes's *The Last Enchantment,* Sylvia Wynter's *The Hills of Hebron,* and H. Orlando Patterson's *The Children of Sisyphus.*

Apart from getting to know these 'pioneers' through the school- and lending-libraries, the reader will be able to experience the added excitement of growing up with these new books at a time when many of their authors are gathering momentum for the first *full* assault of West Indian literature over virtually undiscovered ground, in what is possibly the most fascinating literary debut in modern fiction. Let there be no mistake about this: many of the West Indian writers are establishing their worth in Britain, America, and in Europe in translation, which means that their writing should be of particular significance in the West Indies where, to borrow an expression from the world of popular music, its meaning has 'come to stay' – in the way that the Trinidadian *calypso* and the Jamaican *mento* have come and 'stayed'. It is appropriate, therefore, that some of this material should now be made available for school use and that it should be regarded, along with similar writing from other literatures, as a profitable subject for study.

Finally, I hope that these stories will not only give the reader pleasure but will add something to his understanding of life, and also help him to develop a real and lasting interest in good writing and provide the means by which he can recognize other works of merit. I hope too that, with an increasing critical awareness of what the writers of these and other stories are trying to do, the reader himself will be encouraged more often to write what *he* thinks and feels about the world around him.

ANDREW SALKEY

...A single chain, in the bright geography
Of shoals and bays, like emeralds in a book...

DEREK WALCOTT: from *A Map of the Antilles*

Two People Lived in Me

C. L. R. James

This extract has been taken from C. L. R. James's impressive autobiographical essay Beyond a Boundary *and has been given its present title with the author's permission. In it the West Indian reader can identify some of the specific ingredients which go into the making of a British colonial personality. He will be shown both the good and the harmful effects of a transplanted alien culture on an already 'transplanted' people; the 'mystical' influence of cricket and the highly idiosyncratic style and system of education-for-the-élite as they impinge on a promising young Trinidadian boy in Port of Spain in the early part of this century.*

The Trinidad Government offered yearly free exhibitions from the elementary schools of the island to either of the two secondary schools, the Government Queen's Royal College and the Catholic college, St. Mary's. The number today is over four hundred, but in those days it was only four. Through this narrow gate, boys, poor but bright, could get a secondary education and in the end a Cambridge Senior Certificate, a useful passport to a good job. There were even more glittering prizes. Every year the two schools competed for three island scholarships worth £600 each. With one of these a boy could study law or medicine and return to the island with a profession and therefore independence. There were at that time few other roads to independence for a black man who started without means. The higher posts in the Government, in engineering and other scientific professions were monopolized by white people, and, as practically all big business was also in their hands, the coloured people were, as a rule, limited to the lower posts. Thus law and medicine were the only ways out. Lawyers and doctors made large fees and enjoyed great social prestige. The final achievement was when the Governor nominated one of these coloured men to the Legislative Council to represent the people. To what degree he represented them should not distract us here. We must keep our eye on the course: exhibition, scholarship, profession, wealth, Legislative Council and the title of Honourable. Whenever someone brought it off the local people were very proud of him.

That was the course marked out for me. The elementary-school masters all over the island sought bright boys to train for this examination, and to train a boy for this and win with him was one of the marks of a good teacher. My father was one of the best, and now fortune conspired to give him in his own son one whom he considered the brightest student he had ever had or known. The age limit for the examination was twelve and when I was eight I stopped going to my aunt's for half the year and my father gave me a little extra coaching. On the day of the examination a hundred boys were brought from all parts of the island by their teachers, like so many fighting cocks. That day I looked at the favourites and their trainers with wide-open eyes, for I was a country bumpkin. My father when asked about me always dismissed the enquiry with the remark, 'I only brought him along to get him accustomed to the atmosphere.' This was true, for he had great confidence in himself and in me, and the most we ever did that year was half an

hour extra in the morning and the same in the afternoon. I was only eight and he would not press me. But some weeks afterwards, when the daily paper arrived, I heard him shout to my mother: 'Bessie! Come and look at this!'

I had not won a place, but was among the ten or a dozen boys who gained special mention and had been placed seventh.

'If I had taught you seriously, boy, you would have won,' my father said to me. The next year, though I had still two other chances, I ran away with the examination, came first and at that time was the youngest boy ever to have won a place. Congratulations poured in from all over the island and particularly from the teaching fraternity.

Being Protestant, I naturally went to the Government College. The masters here, too, welcomed me with interest, for these highly trained winners of Government exhibitions formed the best material for defeating the rival college in the annual race for island scholarships, and I was coming in with a reputation second to none. Very soon I attracted public attention again. The British Empire Society or the British Empire League or some such patriotic organization publicized extensively an island-wide essay competition on the British Empire. I sent in my piece and, though there were competitors sixteen and seventeen years of age, I won second prize. (I was given two volumes of Kipling's stories. I could not read or understand them at all for four years. One vacation I picked them up and for two years they supplanted *Vanity Fair* as my perpetual companion. Then I went back to *Vanity Fair*.) The winning of that prize so soon after my brilliant performance in the exhibitioners' examination set the seal on me as a future candidate for the Legislative Council.

It is only now as I write that I fully realize what a ca-
tastrophe I was for all – and there were many – who were
so interested in me. How were they to know that when I put
my foot on the steps of the college building in January 1911
I carried within me the seeds of revolt against all it formally
stood for and all that I was supposed to do in it? My scholastic career was one long nightmare to me, my teachers and
my family. My scholastic shortcomings were accompanied by
breaches of discipline which I blush to think of even today.
But at the same time, almost entirely by my own efforts, I
mastered thoroughly the principles of cricket and of English
literature, and attained a mastery over my own character
which would have done credit to my mother and Aunt
Judith if only they could have understood it. I could not
explain it to their often tear-stained faces for I did not understand it myself. I look back at that little boy with amaze-
ment, and, as I have said, with a gratitude that grows every
day. But for his unshakable defiance of the whole world
around him, and his determination to stick to his own ideas,
nothing could have saved me from winning a scholarship,
becoming an Honourable Member of the Legislative Council
and ruining my whole life.

The first temptation was cricket and I succumbed without
a struggle. On the first day of the term you were invited, if
you wanted to play, to write your name on a paper pinned to
the school notice-board. I wrote down mine. The next day
the names appeared divided into five elevens. The college
had its own ground in the rear of the building and with a
little crowding there was room for five elevens. That afternoon the elevens met and elected their captains. Later, as I
grew older and won my place in the cricket and soccer
elevens, I took my part in the elections of the captains, the

secretaries and the committees. A master presided, but that
was all he did. We managed our own affairs from the fifth
eleven to the first. When I became the secretary I kept a
check on the implements used in all the elevens, wrote down
what was wanted on a sheet of paper, had it signed by a
master and went off to buy them myself for over two hundred boys. We chose our own teams, awarded colours
ourselves, obeyed our captains implicitly. For me it was life
and education.

I began to study Latin and French, then Greek, and much
else. But particularly we learnt (I learnt and obeyed and
taught a code) the English public-school code.

It came doctrinally from the masters, who for two genera-
tions, from the foundation of the school, had been Oxford
and Cambridge men. The striking thing was that inside
the classrooms the code had little success. Sneaking was
taboo, but we lied and cheated without any sense of shame.
I know I did. By common understanding the boys sitting
for the valuable scholarships did not cheat. Otherwise we
submitted, or did not submit, to moral discipline, according
to upbringing and temperament.

But as soon as we stepped on to the cricket or football
field, more particularly the cricket field, all was changed.
We were a motley crew. The children of some white officials
and white business men, middle-class blacks and mulattos,
Chinese boys, some of whose parents still spoke broken
English, Indian boys, some of whose parents could speak
no English at all, and some poor black boys who had won
exhibitions or whose parents had starved and toiled on plots
of agricultural land and were spending their hard-earned
money on giving the eldest boy an education. Yet rapidly
we learned to obey the umpire's decision without question,

B

however irrational it was. We learned to play with the team, which meant subordinating your personal inclinations, and even interest, to the good of the whole. We kept a stiff upper lip in that we did not complain about ill-fortune. We did not denounce failures, but 'Well tried' or 'Hard luck' came easily to our lips. We were generous to opponents and congratulated them on victories, even when we knew they did not deserve it. We lived in two worlds. Inside the classrooms the heterogeneous jumble[1] of Trinidad was battered and jostled and shaken down into some sort of order. On the playing field we did what ought to be done. Every individual did not observe every rule. But the majority of the boys did. The best and most-respected boys were precisely the ones who always kept them. When a boy broke them he knew what he had done, and, with the cruelty and intolerance of youth, from all sides our denunciations poured in on him. Eton or Harrow[2] had nothing on us.

Another source of this fierce, self-imposed discipline were the magazines and books that passed among us from hand to hand: *The Boy's Own Paper,* a magazine called *The Captain,* annuals of which I remember the name of only one: *Young England,* the Mike stories by P. G. Wodehouse and scores of similar books and magazines. These we understood; these we lived by; the principles they taught we absorbed through the pores and practised instinctively. The books we read in class meant little to most of us.

To all this I took as a duck to water. The organizing of boys into elevens, the selection of teams, the keeping of

[1] *the heterogeneous jumble* – A description of the diverse racial mixture of schoolboys in the author's school in Trinidad.
[2] *Eton and Harrow* – Eton College and Harrow School are celebrated English Public Schools.

scores, all that I had been doing at second-hand with Grace[3] and Ranjitsinhji[4] and Trumper[5] I now practised in real life with real people. I read boys' books and magazines, twice as many as any other boy. I knew what was done and what was not done. One day when I bowled three maiden overs in succession and a boy fresh from England said to me, 'James, you must take yourself off now, three maiden overs,' I was disturbed. I had not heard that one before; this boy was from England and so he probably knew.

Before very long I had acquired a discipline for which the only name is Puritan.[6] I never cheated; I never appealed for a decision unless I thought the batsman was out; I never argued with the umpire; I never jeered at a defeated opponent; I never gave to a friend a vote or a place which by any stretch of imagination could be seen as belonging to an enemy or to a stranger. My defeats and disappointments I took as stoically as I could. If I caught myself complaining or making excuses I pulled up. If afterwards I remembered doing it I took an inward decision to try not to do it again. From the eight years of school life this code became the moral framework of my existence. It has never left me. I learnt it

---

[3] *Grace* – Dr W. G. Grace, the great English cricketer who in a career lasting more than forty years scored over 50,000 runs and took nearly 3,000 wickets.

[4] *Ranjitsinhji* – Kumar Shri Ranjitsinhji, later the *Jam Sahib of Nawanagar*, a Rajput, and a famous cricketer. He played for Sussex and England in 1900, making over 3,000 runs with an average of 87. He was also one of the founders of modern batting, by his development of back-play and the leg-glide. He wrote *The Jubilee Book of Cricket*.

[5] *Trumper* – Victor Trumper, a celebrated Australian cricketer, an easy natural batsman who met with astonishing success in the English tours of 1902, 1905, and 1910.

[6] *Puritan* – The term is used here to mean a person of extreme moral rectitude.

as a boy; I have obeyed it as a man and now I can no longer laugh at it. I failed to live up to it at times, but when I did I knew and that is what matters. I had a clue and I cared; I couldn't care more. For many years I was a cricket correspondent in the West Indies, having to write about myself, my own club, my intimate friends and people who hated me. Mistakes in judgment I made often enough, but I was as righteous as the Angel Gabriel, and no one ever challenged my integrity. In order to acquire this code I was driven to evasions, disobedience, open rebelliousness, continuous lies and even stealing.

My business at school was to do my lessons, win prizes and ultimately win the scholarship. Nobody ever doubted that if I wanted to I could. The masters wrote regularly in my reports 'Bad' or 'Good', as the case might be, but usually added, 'Could do much better if he tried'.

I did not try. Without any difficulty I could keep up in school, but an exhibition winner was being paid for by Government money and had to maintain a certain standard. I fell below it. My distracted father lectured me, punished me, flogged me. I would make good resolutions, do well for one term and fall from grace again. Then came a resounding scandal. I was reported to the Board of Education and threatened with the loss of my exhibition. It appeared in the public Press and all the teaching fraternity, who always read the reports of the meetings of the Board, read it, and thus learned what was happening to the prospective scholarship winner and Honourable Member of the Legislative Council. There were family meetings, the whole family, to talk to me and make me see the error of my ways. I was not only ruining my own chances. My godfather was a teacher; Aunt Judith's husband was a teacher; my sister's godfather was a teacher. The James clan had a proud status in the teaching profession; my father was an acknowledged star in that firmament and here was I bringing public disgrace upon him and all of them.

I was given orders to stop playing and get home by a certain train. I just couldn't do it. I would calculate that it would take me twenty-five minutes to catch the train. Then I would think I could do it in twenty; then just one last over and then it was too late to try anyway. I invented beforehand excuses which would allow me to stay and play and take the late train. When I got into the eleven, there were matches on Saturdays. I devised Saturday duties which the masters had asked me to perform; I forged letters; I borrowed flannels; I borrowed money to pay my fare; I borrowed bicycles to ride to the matches and borrowed money to repair them when I smashed them. I was finally entangled in such a web of lies, forged letters, borrowed clothes and borrowed money that it was no wonder that the family looked on me as a sort of trial from heaven sent to test them as Job was tested. There were periods when my father relented and I lived normally. But then bad reports would come, the prohibitions would be re-imposed and I would plan to evade them. I was not a vicious boy. All I wanted was to play cricket and soccer, not merely to play but to live the life, and nothing could stop me. When all my tricks and plans and evasions failed I just went and played.

Two people lived in me: one, the rebel against all family and school discipline and order; the other, a Puritan who would have cut off a finger sooner than do anything contrary to the ethics of the game.

As Time Goes By

Samuel Selvon

'As Time Goes By' is a radically different type of story from those we have come to expect from Samuel Selvon. His reputation in the West Indies and in Britain and America has been established on a large output of the most consistently entertaining and brilliantly comic short stories so far written by a West Indian writer. His contribution to this anthology can hardly be called 'comedic Selvon'; it is, instead, a thought-provoking 'mood piece', which is not without its moments of irreverent Selvonian humour, but which is primarily based on the traditional theme of the backward glance at home after emigration: the view from another country. The story is about the bitter-sweet memories of Trinidadian family life and the new sense of responsibility which can claim the young immigrant in his self-imposed 'exile'.

When you were young you could have sat down sometimes and drawn circles on a sheet of paper – little circles, or big ones – it really doesn't matter – and you could have said that that was life, and known it was true. The struggle to fall in line with our desires, do what everyone else was doing. When you were young, you thought: When I'm a man it's going to be different; I'll lead my own life and do what I want to do.

They used to say: He'll be a great man when he grows up; and pat you on the head, and you glared. And now you wish you were young again.

Pa never died, but he always made you promise to work and mind Ma in case it happened tomorrow. So that you started to think he wouldn't die. But what about the fellow at John John[1] the other night? They thought he was sick when he was groaning, but he died.

It all comes back to you now, in that empty space of time before you drop off to sleep. It's no use believing that work will fill in all your time. No matter if each minute is utilized in strenuous physical effort and mental exercise, there's always that period before sleep comes. A time for thinking, to review the years gone by : pictures of what might have been, and the horrible realization that there's no way out.

There used to be nights with Beethoven and Mozart, and *The Dance of the Hours*. You crept into the drawing room and played the records softly while the others were asleep. You didn't know what it was all about, but the music was soothing and people said it was good to listen to the classics.

You had it all figured out, didn't you? The purpose of life, the shortest distance between two points. From the evenings long ago in the Botanical Gardens, rendezvous in the Hollow, secret trysts with girls, nights slouching in the streets of Port of Spain. You remember now the woman in the black dress selling roast corn in Park Street, and you could even taste the cup of coffee you had in a George Street teashop.

Sure you knew the answers. You were going to America,

[1] *John John* – A district of Port of Spain, where the musical steel drums, used in the popular Trinidadian *calypso* steel bands, were invented. John John is the place where the 'pan' (the steel drum) is manufactured, where 'pan music' (the music played on the drum) is traditionally composed, and where the idea of the orchestration of the *calypso* was first tried out.

and so you could do anything and get away with it. Nights of excitement, dances at the club. It was easy to play the game when you knew there was escape to come. You'd never return until you were rich and powerful, so they'd all look up to you, and you'd be able to pick and choose. It was good, this serious desire to come back only when you could curse whom you wanted, stand on your own feet and laugh at the game.

So that it became almost a pleasure to wake up early in the morning and go to the market for beef, and to tell Pa you'd take care of everything if he died tomorrow. In those last days you were friendly; your step was light; your eyes gleamed. Why not? When you returned it was going to be different.

Three years in America. Three years tasting all the dishes life had to offer. Of course, you knew that it was the same in Trinidad, except that you had the feeling this was a strange country and the past could be forgotten. You'd make a fresh start – oh, but at first you were ambitious! Then the snow lost its freshness and skyscrapers became a common sight. There were lost people in America too, and men with wild, hungry looks; and it wasn't so different as you'd thought at first.

Three years in America. When you lived it up and made merry; life was good. In sober days you shrugged at religion. You had it all worked out, didn't you? There was no god – a god was a metaphysical impossibility. Eating hot dogs and whistling *Rhapsody in Blue* in the subway station, waiting for the train to come in. The sound echoed in the hollow spaces, magnified, came back as if projected in a loudspeaker.

Life was walking in New York with a girl, and she intelligent and understanding. And one night on a bridge she told you this is what George Gershwin saw and heard – the city lighted up with a million lights, the toots of the river boats horn in the foggy night. And you saw it too; the life within the life, the music of the spheres sounded pleasantly in your ears.

But when you felt the cold you cried out, like Pa when he was distressed. You wanted to hate the snow; you huddled and shivered and your bones rattled, and you cried for home and the genial warmth of the tropic sun.

And all the time you were getting no nearer to this wealth you were going to bring back to Trinidad; but Pa, he was getting nearer to his Tomorrow.

So you came back with a Yankee drawl, but when we asked about the cold you broke down and said: *When it hit me so ah bawl for me modder.*

You made us understand that it was only for a holiday, though; you were going back. There was that girl in New York who said she'd wait. This time you just wanted to get away from Trinidad; there was one ambition: to come back with wealth and a profession. You said you'd get a job in New York – hundreds of things to do, you said; a man could use his talent and get paid for it. You were going to settle down in New York, have lunch parties in Greenwich Village with would-be artists and poets.

So this was just a holiday, strengthening your body for the blast of winter. You went around to the clubs, to dances, visited friends and spoke like a Yankee.

I have had the experience, you know, you'd say almost apologetically, enlightening us on certain points; I have been in there, pitching with them, playing ball.

The home-coming lost its lustre, too. Everyone got accustomed to you again – not that you didn't expect it. You knew there'd be a lull, and you prepared for it by letting your letters pile up, so you'd have to spend a long time replying to them all. And you began to exercise, running around the Queen's Park Savannah at nights.

You told them at home that you weren't staying; you were going to live in America. Pa said: 'What about Ma? I may die soon, and there is no one to take care of her.'

But you didn't answer. And then he said there was no money this time, that you'd have to make out yourself.

Even if you did reply, now, staring at the ceiling, there were different answers to make. This was the time, alone in your room in the dark. Thoughts go whirling around in your brain, screaming for escape. And you could hear Pa coughing in his room, and when he retched you knew it was black pudding and souse which fell in the basin. Now was the time to make the decision; now was the time to assess the day's activities, to sift the thoughts and pierce the darkness in your mind. All your past parades before you like pictures on a screen: Port of Spain, Chicago, New York. The faces of people remembered in a particular scene, at a specified time. There were times like this too in New York when you couldn't sleep and just lay there and refused to put order in the chaos of your thoughts. But this time you had to make up your mind....

It started all over again; you had travelled in a circle and there was Pa waiting for you on Saturday nights, groaning and asking you to promise to take care of Ma, as he might die tomorrow. You hadn't expected this; you had thought it was just going to be a holiday in the tropics; and when you were well you'd return to the girl in New York.

Pa said business was bad, and why didn't you stay and help him? *Honour thy father and thy mother.*

It was just as if nothing had happened. You hadn't gone away; you'd been right here all the time. And in the morning you expected that you'd have to get up early and go in the market for beef.

Oh God! you whimpered in the dark.

Sandra Street

Michael Anthony

'Sandra Street' is certainly one of Michael Anthony's most graceful, low-keyed short stories. It is a poignant recollection of a young Trinidadian's life at school, in which his favourite teacher plays the major role in what might be over-emphatically called the 'West Indian class war'.

Mr Blades, the new teacher, was delighted with the compositions we wrote about Sandra Street. He read some aloud to the class. He seemed particularly pleased when he read what was written by one of the boys from the other side of the town.

'Sandra Street is dull and uninteresting,' the boy wrote. 'For one half of its length there are a few houses and a private school (which we go to) but the other half is nothing but a wilderness of big trees.' – Mr Blades smiled from the corners of his mouth and looked at those of us who belonged to Sandra Street. 'In fact,' the boy wrote, 'it is the only street in our town that has big trees, and I do not think it is a part of our town at all because it is so far and so different from our other streets.'

The boy went on to speak of the gay attractions on the other side of the town, some of which, he said, Sandra Street could never dream to have. In his street, for instance, there was the savannah where they played football and cricket, but the boys of Sandra Street had to play their cricket in the road. And to the amusement of Mr Blades who also came from the other side of the town, he described Sandra Street as a silly little girl who ran away to the bushes to hide herself.

Everyone laughed except the few of us from Sandra Street, and I knew what was going to happen when school was dismissed, although Mr Blades said it was all a joke and in fact Sandra Street was very fine. I didn't know whether he meant this or not, for he seemed very much amused and I felt this was because he came from the other side of the town.

He read out a few more of the compositions. Some of them said very nice things about Sandra Street but those were the ones written by ourselves. Mr Blades seemed delighted about these, too, and I felt he was trying to appease us when he said that they showed up a new character of the beauty of Sandra Street. There were only a few of us who were appeased, though, and he noticed this and said all right, next Tuesday we'll write about the other side of the town. This brought fiendish laughter from some of us from Sandra Street, and judging from the looks on the faces of those from the other side of the town, I knew what would happen next Tuesday, too, when school was dismissed. And I felt that whatever happened it wasn't going to make any difference to our side or to the other side of the town.

Yet the boy's composition was very truthful. Sandra Street was so different from the other streets beyond. Indeed, it came from the very quiet fringes and ran straight up to the forests. As it left the town there were a few houses and shops along it, and then the school, and after that there were not many more houses, and the big trees started from there till the road trailed off to the river that bordered the forests. During the day all was very quiet except perhaps for the voice of one neighbour calling to another, and if some evenings brought excitement to the schoolyard, these did very little to disturb the calmness of Sandra Street. Nor did the steel-band gently humming from the other side of the town. I had to remember the steel-band because although I liked to hear it I had to put into my composition that it was very bad. We had no steel-bands in Sandra Street, and I thought I could say this was because we were decent, cultured folk and didn't like the horrible noises of steel-bands.

I sat in class recalling the boy's composition again. Outside the window I could see the women coming out of the shops. They hardly passed each other without stopping to talk and this made me laugh. For that was exactly what the boy had written – that they couldn't pass without stopping to talk, as if they had something to talk about.

I wondered what they talked about. I did not know. What I did know was that they never seemed to leave Sandra Street to go into the town. Maybe they were independent of the town. I chuckled, a triumphant little chuckle because this, too, would be good to put into my composition next Tuesday.

Dreamingly I gazed out of the window. I noticed how Sandra Street stood away from the profusion of houses. Indeed, it didn't seem to belong to the town at all. It stood off, not proudly, but sadly, like one desiring peace and rest. I felt all filled-up inside. Not because of the town in the distance, but because of this strange little road. It was funny, the things the boy had written; he had written in anger what I thought of now in joy. He had spoken of the pleasures and palaces on the other side of the town. He had

said why they were his home sweet home. As I looked at
Sandra Street I knew, too, why it was my home sweet home.
It was dull and uninteresting to him but it meant so much
to me. It was—

'Oh!' I started, as the hand rested on my shoulder.

'It's recess,' said Mr Blades.

'Oh! – yes, Sir.' The class was surging out to the play-
ground. I didn't seem to have heard a sound before.

Mr Blades looked at me and smiled. 'What are you
thinking of?' he said.

He seemed to be watching inside me. Inside my very
mind. I stammered out a few words which even if they
were clear wouldn't have meant anything. I stopped. He
was still smiling quietly at me. 'You are the boy from
Sandra Street?' he said.

'Yes, Sir.'

'I thought so,' he said.

What happened on the following Tuesday after school
was a lot worse than what had ever happened before, and
it was a mystery how the neighbours didn't complain or
Mr Blades didn't get to hear of it. We turned out to school
the next morning as if all had been peaceful, and truly there
was no sign of the battle save the little bruises which were
easy to explain away.

We kept getting compositions to write. Mr Blades was
always anxious to judge what we wrote but none gave him
as much delight as those we had written on Sandra Street.
He had said that he knew the other side of the town very
well and no one could fool him about that, but if any boy
wrote anything about Sandra Street he would have to see it.
And when he had said that, he had looked at me and I

was very embarrassed. I had turned my eyes away, and he had said that when the mango season came he would see the boy who didn't speak the truth about Sandra Street.

Since that day I was very shy of Mr Blades and whenever I saw him walking towards me I turned in another direction. At such times there would always be a faint smile at the corners of his mouth.

I stood looking out of the school window one day thinking about this and about the compositions when again I felt a light touch and jumped.

'Looking out?' Mr Blades said.

'Yes, Sir.'

He stood there over me and I did not know if he was looking down at me or looking outside, and presently he spoke.

'Hot, eh?'

'Yes,' I said.

He moved in beside me and we both stood there looking out of the window. It was just about noon and the sun was blazing down on Sandra Street. The houses stood there tall and almost sombre and there seemed to be no movement about save for the fowls lying in the shadows of the houses. As I watched this, a certain sadness came over me and I looked over the houses across to the hills. Suddenly my heart leaped and I turned to Mr Blades, but I changed my mind and did not speak. He had hardly noticed that I looked up at him. I saw his face looking sad as his eyes wandered about the houses. I felt self-conscious as he looked at the houses for they were no longer new and the paint had been washed off them by the rains and they had not been re-painted. Then, too, there were no gates and no fences around them as there were in the town, and sometimes, with a great flurry, a hen would scamper from under one house to another leaving dust behind in the hot sun.

I looked at Mr Blades. He was smiling faintly. He saw me me looking at him. 'Fowls,' he said.

'There are no gates,' I apologized.

'No, there are no gates.' And he laughed softly to himself.

'Because—' I had to stop. I didn't know why there were no gates.

'Because you did not notice that before.'

'I noticed that before,' I said.

Looking sharply at me he raised his brows and said slowly. 'You noticed that before. Did you put that in your composition? You are the boy from Sandra Street, are you not?'

'There are more from Sandra Street—'

'Did you notice the cedar grove at the top?' he went on. 'You spoke of the steel-band at the other side of the town; did you speak of the river? Did you notice the hills?'

'Yes.'

'Yes?' His voice grew sterner and more acid. His eyes seemed burning up from within.

'You noticed all this and you wrote about Sandra Street without mentioning it, eh? How many marks did you make?'

'Forty-five.'

He looked surprised. 'I gave you forty-five for writing about steel-band noises and the dirty trams of the town? Look!' he pointed. 'Do you see?'

'Mango blossoms,' I said, feeling to cry out: *I wanted to show it to you.*

c

'Did you write about it?'

'No.' I just wanted to break out and run away from him.

He bent down to me. His face looked harder now, though kind, but I could see there was a fury inside him.

'There is something like observation, Steve,' he said. 'Observation. You live in Sandra Street. Yet Kenneth writes a composition on your own place better than you.'

'He said Sandra Street was soppy,' I cried.

'Of course he said it was soppy. It was to his purpose. He comes from the other side of the town. What has he got to write on? Gaudy houses with gates like prisons around them? High walls cramping the imagination? The milling crowd with faces impersonal as stone hurrying on buses, hurrying off trams. Could he write about that? He said Sandra Street was soppy. Did you prove it wasn't so? Where is your school and his, for instance?'

I was a little alarmed. Funny how I didn't think of that point before. 'Here,' I said. 'In Sandra Street.'

'Did you mention that?'

Mercifully, as he was talking the school bell sounded. The fowls, startled, ran out into the hot sun across the road. The dust rose, and above the dust, above the houses, the yellow of mango blossom caught my eye.

'The bell, Sir.'

'Yes, the bell's gone. What is it – Geography?'

'Yes, Sir.' And as I turned away he was still standing looking out into the road.

It was long before any such thing happened again. Though often when it was dry and hot I stood at the window looking out; I watched the freedom of the fowls between the tall houses, and sometimes the women talked to each other through the windows and smiled. I noticed, too, the hills which were now streaked with the blossoms of the poui[1], and exultantly I wondered how many people observed this and knew it was a sign of the rains. None of the mango blossoms could be seen now, for they had already turned into fruit, and I knew how profuse they were because I had been to the hills.

I chuckled to myself. There is something like observation, Steve! And how I wished Mr Blades would come to the window again that I could tell him what lay between the mango trees in the hills.

I knew that he was not angry with me. I realized that he was never angry with any boy because of the district the boy came from. We grew to like him, for he was very cheerful, though mostly he seemed dreamy and thoughtful. That is except at composition time.

He really came to life then. His eyes would gleam as he read our compositions and whenever he came to a word he did not like he would frown and say any boy was a sissy to use such a word. And if a composition pleased him he would praise the boy and be especially cheerful with him, and the boy would be proud and the rest of us would be jealous and hate him.

I was often jealous. Mr Blades had a passion for compositions, and I was anxious to please him to make up for that day at the window. I was anxious to show him how much I observed and often I noted new things and put them into my compositions. And whenever I said something wonder-

[1] *poui* – A large, colourful hard wood tree from which the 'poui-stick' is cut and used stylishly by promenading boys and young men in the streets of Port of Spain.

ful I knew it because of the way Mr Blades would look at me, and sometimes he would take me aside and talk to me. But many weeks ran out before we spoke at the window again.

I didn't start this time because I was expecting him. I had been watching him from the corners of my eyes.

'The sun's coming out again,' he said.

'It's cloudy,' I said.

The rains had almost ceased but there were still great patches of dark cloud in the sky. When the wind blew they moved slowly and clumsily, but if the sun was free of one there would be another. The sun was shining brightly now, although there was still a slight drizzle of rain, and I could smell the steam rising from the hot pitch and from the galvanized roofs.

'Rain falling, sun shining,' Mr Blades said. And I remembered what they said about that and I smiled and when Mr Blades pressed me to tell him I laughed and would not say. Then thoughtfully he said, 'You think they're all right?'

'What, Sir?'

'In the 'mortelle² root.'

I was astonished. I put my hands to my mouth. How did he know?

He smiled down at me. 'You won't be able to jump over now!'

And the whole thing was revealed. I couldn't help laughing. I had put into my composition how I went into the hills last Sunday evening and how the mango trees were laden with small mangoes, some full, and how there were

---

² *immortelle* – a large shade tree bearing composite blooms of papery texture retaining their colour after being dried; often used to adorn graves.

banana trees among the immortelles and poui. I had spoken
too about the bunch of green bananas I had hidden to ripen
and how afterwards I had jumped across the river to the
other bank.

'They're all right,' I said, and I pretended to be watching
the steam rising from the hot pitch.

'I like bananas,' said Mr Blades. I was sure that he licked
his lips as he looked towards the hills.

I was touched. I felt as one with him. I liked bananas too.
It always made me lick my lips. I thought now of the
whole bunch which must be yellow by now between the
immortelle roots.

'Sir —' I said to him, and I hesitated. Then I took the
wild chance. And when he answered a feeling of extreme
happiness swept over me.

I remember that evening as turning out bright, almost
blinding. The winds had pushed away the heavy clouds and
the only evidence of the rains were the little puddles along
Sandra Street. I remember the hills as being strange in an
enchanted sort of way, and I felt the enchantment came
mainly from Mr Blades being with me. We watched the
leaves of the cocoa gleaming with the moisture of the rains,
and Mr Blades confessed he never thought there was so
much cocoa in the hills. We watched the cyp,[3] too, profuse
between the laden mango trees, and the redness of their
rain-picked flowers was the redness of blood.

We came to the immortelle tree where I had hidden the
bananas. I watched to see if Mr Blades licked his lips but he
did not. He wasn't even watching.

'Sir,' I said in happy surprise, after removing the covering
of trash from the bunch. Mr Blades was gazing across the

[3] cyp – An affectionate abbreviation for a type of cypress tree in Trinidad.

trees. I raised my eyes. Not far below, Sandra Street swept by, bathed in light.

'The bananas, Sir,' I said.

'Bananas!' he cried, despairingly. 'Bananas are all you see around you, Steve?'

I was puzzled. I thought it was that we had come to the hills for.

'Good Heavens!' he said with bitterness. 'To think that *you* instead of Kenneth should belong to Sandra Street.'

The Bitter Choice

Clifford Sealy

This moving story touches on the traditional conflict between privilege and deprivation. Sealy's world is the anguish of the Trinidadian unemployed who have always sat in Woodford Square and talked endlessly among themselves, despairing and envying and never coming either to a personal resolution or to the means of influencing a public decision about their own misery and dejection.

The oppressive midday heat beat fiercely down upon the withered blades of grass in Woodford Square,[1] the airy sanctuary of the intelligentsia of Port of Spain's unemployed. Unequal groups of ragged, melancholic, and vociferous men and women scattered themselves over the parched tract discussing one subject or another.

In one group, the absorbing subject was foreign politics; in another, careful consideration was being given to counsel's submissions in a case of murder then being heard; and in a third, the Government's intervention in the existing water-front workers' strike was being animatedly debated.

There were as many topics of conversation as there were groups; and these topics were as varied in nature and enormity as the men who discussed them were in character and appearance. In the centre of the Square rose a small, green metal statue, encircled by a wide stone pond which

[1] *Woodford Square* – A popular square or 'open lot' in Port of Spain; a haunt for 'park orators', unemployed men and passers-by; similar to the park at Parade and the Race Course in Kingston, Jamaica.

was invariably empty. And facing this pond were six wooden benches whose coat of deep brown paint had long since vanished, exposing the rough yellow pitch-pine.

On one of these benches sat three men. Leo was in the middle. Tall and sturdy, he wore a faded and dirty khaki suit, which, by the vast areas of his arms and legs it left uncovered, gave evidence of an earlier association with a shorter and slimmer owner.

On Leo's right sat Eric. Lean and emaciated, his bones seemed to protrude through his thin, black skin, and a crafty glint shone in his ashen eyes.

Sam completed the triumvirate.[2] Short and slim, he was the least prepossessing, and his opinions always drifted between those of his two comrades.

'I hear the Government want people for stevedore work, boys,' Eric ventured in a hoarse and insinuating tone.

Leo blew a thick cloud of smoke through his heavy, frog-like lips. Then, with the tip of the little finger of his right hand he flicked the grey ash from the end of his cigarette, lightly crushed out the dim red glow on the iron arm-rest of the bench, brushed away the black cinders and placed the still warm 'zoot' behind his right ear.

He did not speak; nor did Sam, who with lowered head watched his stumpy fingers play with a loose shirt-button.

'What happen, now?' growled Eric, injured by this un-anticipated silence. 'All you ain't want work or what? The Government giving we work, and all you sitting down like all you proud!'

[2] *triumvirate* – (Latin: *triumviratus*, from *trium virorum*, of three men). In the days of Imperial Rome a triumvirate was the office or magistracy of a triumvir (one of three officers mutually exercising the same public function); it was also the government of three joint officers, or a coalition of three magistrates or rulers in a joint administration.

Leo was angered by Eric's sarcasm; and facing his companion, he shouted with a vehemence born of deep moral conviction, 'We black people ain't have no unity! Anybody who take that kind of work want shooting! When the white man have he business, all of them does get together. But when we black people do something, the other set does get against them! We ain't have no unity, that is what!' he concluded, turning around again and wiping his oval, unshaven face with the sleeve of his jacket.

'You right, *oui*, Leo! You right, boy!' Sam chimed in uncertainly. 'We black people really ain't have no love for one another. That is the real, real truth!'

'Don't mind Leo and he stupidness, man, Sam!' came Eric's admonishing voice. 'He minding them politicians and their talk!'

'But what the man say yesterday is true, though,' Leo put in.

'What he say? I wish I mind them and their talk! That ain't going to get you any place!' Rising from the bench and dusting the seat of his trousers with the palm of his hand, Eric continued, his crooked features contorting themselves into a contemptuous grimace: 'Black people too damn foolish.' And with a condescending pat on Leo's shoulder, he said as he departed, somewhat with the air of a wizened father to an imprudent son, 'What you say is true; but politics ain't for black people. Man have to live.'

Leo watched the lanky, half-stooping figure walk down the pathway, and he felt strangely towards him. Eric was depraved; that he knew. Yet, his words always inspired for themselves a queer respect in Leo's mind.

There was much activity in the Square at this hour. Shop assistants hurried backwards and forwards, going to and from their lunch. And there were also the shoppers: women, stout and thin, tall and short, with parcels hanging from their arms and gossip clinging to their tongues.

The clock of neighbouring Trinity Cathedral chimed twelve. It reminded Leo that soon he would have to face Mabel, his wife, who came from Grenada. The thought of Mabel sent his mind rolling backwards to the events of the past few days.

Life was hard. Life, he reflected, had never been rosy; now, however, it was coarse and horrid. And Mabel's callousness worsened matters. And slender hope there was of her changing since she had joined the 'In Jesus Mighty Name' sect, a band of misguided poor people, who each in his distress fancied he had received a 'call' to block the street corners at nights with prayer meetings.

Returning from her 'lecture' yesterday afternoon, he recalled, she was distressingly hostile.

'When you going to get work, Leo?' she had asked him. 'Is over a whole year you ain't working. How long you think we could live so?'

'But, Mabel,' he had reproached her, 'I trying my best. Some people ain't working for years, now.'

'That is some people,' she had heatedly exploded, 'but me is me. I can't go on living like this, not knowing what I go eat tomorrow, or when the man going to put we out for the rent, or borrowing and not knowing when I am going to pay back. This ain't go do.'

'Keep courage, *doudou*,'[3] he had exhorted her, adding in

---

[3] *doudou* – *Doux doux* or *doo doo*: a term of endearment: like 'darling'.

an effort to mitigate her depression, 'you forget is tomorrow I have to see the man at the Soap Factory.'

Sam's squeaky voice drew Leo out of his meditations. 'What about the job you was to get this morning, Leo? You ain't tell me nothing about it.'

'The foreman's cousin already get it, man!' Leo told him.

'God-father, boy,' Sam murmured understandingly, shaking his odd, round head from left to right, 'God-father in everything, *oui.*'

Presently, the number of persons travelling through the Square lessened, and the clouds of dust kicked up by their hasty steps dispersed. Occasionally, a bunch of baked and cracked leaves would lazily float to the ground; while above, the soft kissing of the trees could be heard.

Some of the groups broke up; but almost immediately, new ones formed themselves in the same spots. Others, overcome by the scorching glare of the sun, sought shelter in the small, concrete bandstand. But the Square, then, as at all times throughout the day, retained its minimum population of fifty idle souls.

'We going see, tomorrow, old man,' said Leo, rising from his seat.

'All right,' Sam said.

Soon, Leo arrived at his barrack-room[4] in Duncan Street. Mabel was lying on the small iron bed, her cheap, green spotted dress combining picturesquely with the variegated colours of the fibre mattress. In her fat hands, wrinkled by continual laundering, reposed an expensively bound, black Bible.

Disappointment must clearly have been reflected in Leo's

---

[4] *barrack-room* – A tenement room.

anguished features, for at sight of him, Mabel exclaimed, 'You ain't get the job!'

'No!' Leo said.

'But this is ...' Mabel burst out, closing her Bible and rising to a sitting position. 'What you mean by? If you know you can't get work, what you take wife for?'

His pride severely wounded, Leo spluttered, 'But, Mabel, I trying me best.'

'You trying you' best,' she sneered. 'How Jane's husband working on the wharf three days now?'

'He is a dog, you see!' growled Leo, getting up from the small wooden bench on which he sat, and which together with a dully varnished bureau and a rectangular dining-table comprised the entire household furniture. 'I ain't want no work like that. He ...'

'Oh-ho, you' picking and choosing,' she snarled, burying the knuckles of her fingers deeply into her sides. 'You minding them Unions and their politics. I see. Is pride that have you going on so.'

'It ain't pride. Is education. Education like the people in ...'

'Education what! Education could mind you?'

'You ain't understand ...'

'I understand, well. You ain't really want work. But I ain't living with no man who ain't want to work and mind his wife. I ain't any woman you just find, and you have to mind me.' And with an air of dramatic finality, she added 'If you ain't want to mind me, I go do it myself.'

'What happen?'

'I'm very calm,' Mabel replied, her beady black eyes glistening with defiance, 'but if you ain't mind me, other people going to do it.'

'Go to hell,' he shouted, tumbling out of the room.

A huge and excited crowd had gathered in Prince Street.
Men and women stood in the streets and on the pavements
noisily speaking to each other. Some of them wore bands of
various colours on their sleeveless arms; some held in their
hands small galvanized buckets filled with water or cane-
baskets filled with food; others waved small cardboard
placards splashed with bold red.

To Leo there was an infectious exultancy that seemed
more appropriate to a Carnival sailors' band. He marvelled
at the ease with which they fell into the military march and
the unrestrained zeal with which they swung their banners.

As though to accentuate the incongruity of the assembly,
there stood at the head a few smartly dressed men, sporting
expensive ties.

'Them is big shots,' Leo thought to himself. 'Them ain't
stevedores.'

Then the ungainly crowd began to move, and Leo
found himself involuntarily moving with them. The in-
distinct babbling ceased. Placards rose high in the air and
voices shouted to the heavens.

Starting at first in the front, the song swiftly spread
through the assembly like a summer fire in a dense forest.

'Sing, comrade, sing,' a burly bare-foot picket commanded Leo, shoving him against the back of a formidable
looking *marchande*.[5]

The street reverberated with the shuffling of their steps
and the sound of their voices, as bass blended with soprano
into one soul-gripping symphony.

[5] *marchande* – A market woman.

Hold the fort for we are coming
Union men be strong

The words which came rapidly to Leo found a dim echo deep within his breast which, as he marched and sang, rose to a choking crescendo.

He stumbled out of the demonstration and stood at the corner of Prince and Henry Streets in order to catch his breath. Many persons were standing on the pavements and one of these he heard comment to another, 'If they would only maintain this solidarity, they'll surely win.'

Leo turned round and noticed that the speaker was a tall, neatly dressed, bespectacled youth with a tuft of beard concealing his chin. For a moment Leo's eyes were imprisoned by the glare of the young man's shining pair of shoes; and he could not resist a cynical chuckle as he looked at his own dirty, red-spotted alpargatas[6] through whose narrow mouths his unwashed toes protruded.

Leo's soul became enmeshed in a disturbing emotional conflict. Thoughts of Mabel and her threat, of Eric and his remarks, of his own hunger, of the leaders of the demonstration, of the teachers, of the strike, and of his now unendurable and apparently purposeless existence were all, in some curious way, united in his brain.

He walked down Henry Street, away from the multitude. away from the contagious joy which reminded him of himself, away, away. Vaguely, as though through a mist, he saw and avoided the cars and carts which obstructed his route.

Eventually, he reached South Quay. A line of men were standing in front of a large, wooden building. Even this

---

[6] *alpargatas* – Casual footwear. Heelless, open-toed sandals with woven corded uppers and leather soles.

sight did not inspire him with hope. He was too weak. Yet he did not stop to ask any questions but drew instinctively closer to the line.

'Psst, Leo!' came a hoarse, familiar whisper. 'Look, a room in here!'

Spinning round, his face flushed for a moment, Leo hesitated. He turned to leave. But before he could move, Eric's long hand had gripped him.

'Come, you young fool, come in here before you lose your chance,' Eric said.

For one deep, significant moment, Leo resisted Eric's tugging. He seemed totally paralysed as his contradictory thoughts revolved in one maddening, ever-narrowing circle. He felt them racing to a challenging climax. And when it came, he chose.

Squeezing himself behind Eric, he hardly heard the latter covetously whisper to him, 'Is three dollars a day the Government giving we! Black people too damn foolish!'

'Uh-huh!' was Leo's laconic reply.

The Preacher

George Lamming

'The Preacher' is taken from George Lamming's first novel
In the Castle of My Skin, *and has been given its title by
the editor with the permission of the author. It is a self-
contained extract from one of the great novels in West
Indian literature. Like the rest of the story from which it is
taken, 'The Preacher' is about the 'education in public' of
a whole village. The preacher at the crossroads is yet
another teacher and a very definite formative influence in
the life of at least one young Barbadian villager.*

When night fell it was as though the darkness had dropped
from the sky. At four o'clock the sun appearing to move
towards the sea shone from the west with a scarlet brilliance
and the white marl roads gleamed. The wind had gone
away and the trees were steady. At this hour the village
had seemed unreally still. Sky, trees, wind, clouds: all
these things which earlier had seemed immediate were now
remote and inactive. There were no clouds at all and the
sky deeply curved looked hard and solid. The sun bleeding
its light over the land seemed to hang on to the sky as
though it were a foreign and unwanted body. The trees
resembled the lamp-posts in their carriage, upright, steady
and stupid, and the houses scotched[1] on the groundsels of
limestone, neutral and resigned. At one corner in the shade
of the mahogany trees an old woman sat behind a tray of

[1] *scotched* – Squatted in the smallest possible space.

oranges, plums and nuts. The tray was placed on a bench the shape and size of the one she sat on. She wore a white head tie and a blue apron. She was asleep, her head drooping forward, the chin lazily closeted in the sink of the neck, and her lips hanging loose and slack. A small boy nestled near her, stole a plum from the tray and stuffed his mouth before dropping his head in a nod to the ground. The old woman half-opened her eyes, scratched her ears and mumbled something to the boy. He didn't answer. She passed her hand along his head and closed her eyes again. The boy waited, then looked up and lifted a banana from the stem. Then he stuffed his pockets with more plums and nuts, not more on the whole than a penny's worth. He quickly rearranged the bananas, shuffled the plums and nuts into a new heap and sat down quietly. Another glance at the old woman and soon he had circled the trees and was out of sight. No one noticed. The old woman slept, and in her sleep on the wooden bench she was like the houses, old and weary and remote.

But out of these bodies which seemed lifeless there had grown others that at other times turned the air into a battle front of flashing light. The high wall which ran through a great part of the village, separating one set of tenants from another, bore bits of bottle along the top, and the light from the green edges seemed to cut through the air. Also many of the houses were roofed with galvanized sheets of iron, and the reflected light seemed to rebound from these into the light that leapt from the broken bottles along the high wall. In the distance the trees seemed steady as before, but nearer one noticed that the branches wavered slightly, and occasionally the leaves were disturbed. At four o'clock the air was a blinding shimmer, the village an unbounded arena

D

where the light contended. At five o'clock there was only shade. The galvanized sheets of iron and the broken bottles looked a dull unreflecting grey over the houses and the high wall. Gradually the leaves seemed to take on the colour of the light, and between the branches the open spaces seemed to be filled up with grey. The twilight was deepening and the street lamps at the corner went on. Lamps were lit in some of the houses, but one knew rather than felt the presence of this light. From now on there was this gradual collision of light, the receding light of day and the light of the gas lamps and the house lamps coming to life. The old woman had steadied the tray on her head, balanced the benches over one arm and walked away. The twilight was deepening into a thicker darkness. And suddenly as if at a signal for action the gas lamps seemed to shine with an aggressive steadiness and the house lamps blazed. The take-over was in the nature of a new beginning. The lamps in the shops went on, and there was movement about the lamp-posts at the corner. The light came out from all the windows and the shapes and the ringed posts at the corner. It heightened the darkness of the land and the sky which now seemed over-crowded with stars. It was six o'clock. It was night.

But there was another light less assertive than the gas lamps. At the crossing where the roads made four, a small gathering of worshippers stood in a circle round a table. There was a white table cloth over the table and on the cloth a green bottle that held a candle in its neck. The candle gave a flame that leapt up and down in the wind. At the centre beside the table the leader sat giving instructions for worship. There were quite a few spectators among whom were Trumper, Boy Blue and myself with another boy who stood very near the circle of worshippers. We were quiet and curious as the leader talked to the others about the proceedings. We had come early in the hope of getting away before the crowd came. The preacher paid us no attention, but the boy whom we didn't know was engrossed in conversation with one of the women. The women were in the majority and they called each other sister. Sister Jones and Sister Bell. There were the men who were referred to as Brother. Brother Franklin and Brother Low. The preacher was Brother Dickson, tall, big-boned and aggressive, with a black face and large hands. Trumper said we should move farther away from the worshippers since they had a way of getting into the spirit. When they got into the spirit they danced and shouted in a strange language. It was the act of speaking in tongues. And when the spirit was more than they could control they insisted by force that those who stood nearby should help to bear the burden of this new energy. We walked a pace or two farther away and waited. At a signal from the leader the worshippers knelt and prayed in silence. As if by silent agreement and long practice their prayers were of equal length, and they got up together intoning a low amen. Then the women sat, some on benches, others on chairs, while the men stood washing their hands in the air and moving their lips in broad, benevolent smiles. Suddenly a woman stepped forward brandishing a tambourine and screamed a hymn. She shook the tambourine and her hips with passionate glee, and Trumper whispered to me that she would soon get the spirit. We couldn't follow the words of the hymn, but the worshippers whose ears were trained recognized the hymn and joined her. Another woman stepped forward in a similar way with her tambourine. Then another and another. The

instruments flashed in the candle-light as the sound rocketed
to the sky. The open-air meeting had begun. The spectators
had increased. When the noise was heard they came from
all parts to join in the singing. The crowd came in a steady
flow as the voices and the tambourines pealed through the
night. The hymn finished, the leader walked over to the
small boy and said something about his soul. The boy
seemed willing but frightened. All eyes were turned in his
direction. This was what the spectators had come for. They
liked to see how others got saved, and sometimes they heard
their testimonies which were often embarrassingly intimate.
Their candour was a sign of their purge, and they confessed
without question the sins they had committed in thought,
word and particularly the deeds that related to the flesh.
The small boy was resisting. The preacher said something
again about the soul and the boy dropped his head. His
resistance was weakening. The preacher made mention of
the wrath of God, and the worshippers expressed their
sorrow in a low drawn-out groan. The boy seemed terribly
frightened and penitent. The preacher held his hand and
the women knelt intoning a hymn of initiation.

'Will you stay tonight?' the preacher asked, and the
crowd was quiet.

'I can't,' the boy said quickly, but it wasn't a direct
refusal. He was frightened. The preacher seemed very hope-
ful and repeated the question. The boy shook his head and
the preacher let go of his hand.

'But you must, my son, you must.' His manner was tender
and solicitous. His voice unsteady and almost broken with
concern. It was amazing how he seemed to melt into a
single emotion: this concern for the other's salvation.

'Don't harden your heart,' he said. 'It's better when you're young; your sins are fewer; and if you're cut off without warning forgiveness is easier.'

The preacher had taken a step back and he seemed to address his words to everybody. Trumper nudged Boy Blue and said it was time for us to leave. 'Seven is the age your eyes are opened,' the preacher said. 'You become responsible. You're past seven now, and if you were called home tonight, you would have to answer that call yourself. You have crossed beyond the boundary of innocence, no father, no mother, godfather or godmother. You are alone, naked in sin, and you must accept and be saved before it's too late. Salvation through Christ is the key to heaven.'

'Yes,' the boy said, 'but the candle frightens me so.' The boy shivered. The preacher looked round at the light that lengthened out over the faces of the worshippers. He seemed puzzled by what the boy had said, for there was nothing about the candle to frighten anyone. The women waited anxious. 'You see,' the boy said, 'the candle makes me remember Elvirah[2] and what she does do. She does burn candle to keep away the spirits 'cause she's Roman

---

[2] Elvirah is not a character in the novel *In the Castle of My Skin*, by George Lamming (published by Michael Joseph Ltd., 1953); she is really a 'presence', a symbolic reference. In fact, she might well be any Roman Catholic Barbadian villager who 'does burn candle ... to burn away the spirits'. She is that person who is usually observed from a distance and is for ever being talked about. In time, her name becomes associated with a special kind of religious behaviour-pattern: the 'burning of candles' for example. In other words, Elvirah is an archetypal figure. Non-Catholic children would naturally be impressed by the village myth surrounding her, and would refer to her, in awe, from time to time. In this scene at the crossroads, Brother Dickson's burning candle, a mere fragmentary symbol of *coincidental* Roman Catholic ritual, is seen through the eyes of the author's non-Catholic boy simply and without prejudice as that which Elvirah 'does do'.

Catholic, as they say they got to burn away the spirits.' There were tears in his eyes and the preacher seemed deeply moved.

'Good Lord be merciful,' he said. 'Spare the innocent from the guiles of Lucifer,[3] and show them the way.' He was remarkably eloquent and he kept a special language to meet every new situation. The boy was going to cry. The preacher's hands were clasped to his neck and his head thrown back so that his chin pointed skyward and the white of his eyes showed dull. He brought his head down sharply and fixed his eyes on the boy in an expression of deep distress.

'The candle won't help her,' he said, 'for it's not the candle that matters. It's the light, the light of the Anointed shed through grace upon the blackness of man's heart. When you see the light, you'll forget the candle and the evil of those who worship images. They are false gods. We have no false gods, only one God, the god who sent His Son and Saviour Jesus Christ to the world to die for our sins. Those who carry candles have never seen the light. They are the disciples of the evil one. And it's this you can be spared from if you stay tonight, see the light and be born again, a living soul and a new man in Christ!'

The preacher knelt in the dust and held the boy's hands tightly in his. Their hands shook, but the boy seemed more deeply shaken by the other's supplication, and his knees responding mechanically to the prayer knelt too. They knelt together on the marl road within the circle which the worshippers had made round the table. We were engrossed and Trumper who had been urging us to leave understood and

[3] *guiles of Lucifer* – The many cunning ways of the Devil.

remained. They had drawn nearer to the table, and the preacher's face shone without reflection, black and wet like bronze in a fine drizzle. His skin was coarse, his fingers thick and tough. I seemed to feel the clutch that kept the boy transfixed to the ground, a prisoner in the light, condemned to be saved, to be free from the evil one, free from the flesh and the whole world of profane longing. The preacher spoke as they knelt. Three or four of the gathering had knelt making a small circle round the boy and the preacher. Kneeling there they seemed in a way to have lined up against him. It was a conspiracy of prayer in the cause of his salvation. The clasp of the man's hand gave the feeling of a closed door through which there would never be escape, and the man's face in its attitude of prayer seemed other than nose, eyes, ears, bone and flesh. I closed my eyes against it, and when I couldn't hear the voices or failed to make sense of the prayers I saw the face solitary and wet and black like bronze in a fine drizzle. The preacher paused, and suddenly spoke again, hardly parting his lips.

'Will you stay tonight?'

The boy bowed his head low to the ground and remained there resigned and submissive. The women sang the hymn of initiation and the preacher stood exhausted but satisfied.

'We better go now,' said Trumper, ' 'cause 'tis 'bout this time the lights go on when anythin' happenin'.' He brought his head close to mine so that his words might not be overheard. The boy was still kneeling beside the preacher incapable of further resistance. They had become the spectacle for everybody's gaze. Those who were there when the boy knelt with the preacher were anxious to see what was going to happen, and those who came late pushed forward through the crowd to see who it was. There was a quiet buzzing as they looked trying to recognize the convert, and the buzzing grew louder with the low murmur of the worshippers. Then it died down and everyone was quiet, waiting to see what would happen next.

Trumper put his head close to Boy Blue's and whispered what he had said to me. Boy Blue smiled and went on looking at the preacher and the boy. Trumper elbowed him again, and Boy Blue made a noise. The man who stood beside him made a sign with his finger, and Boy Blue turned serious. Trumper spoke again. 'You gettin' frighten', Boy Blue said, not turning his head to speak. 'It ain't that I 'fraid,' said Trumper, 'but we gotta go now 'cause it gettin' late. It ain't no sense going when everythin' at a big pitch 'cause you don't know what gone before.' He held his head down as he spoke. 'We gotta go.'

One of the women who sat in the circle near the table looked up and frowned. Trumper was silent. The woman kept her head down for a while, but we knew from the look on her face that she would soon look up again. She seemed to bite her lips as she stared down and across at the preacher and the boy. We wanted to go, but we also wanted to see what would happen to the boy, and it probably wouldn't have been long before the preacher would turn to us to put questions about our salvation. Behind us the crowds had grown thicker and it was always difficult on such occasions to force a way out. Moreover we were secretly ashamed to let the others see us leaving. This always happened at the open-air meeting and in the big church. If you got up to leave before the service was finished people stared at you till you were out of sight. It made you feel shamefully rebellious as though you were turning in disrespect against what you had seen. At the open-air meeting it was likely that the preacher would stand and say what he thought about such behaviour. The priest wouldn't have interrupted the service to make a comment on anything, but the preacher took no chances with the unsaved. If he could persuade them by first making them a public example of cowards, then he would do so. And often it worked, and he thought it good for them. There was nothing to be ashamed of in salvation, and salvation was more urgent than anything else. Trumper elbowed me in the ribs and made a sign with his head. He seemed irritated now by our delay. 'We gotta go now,' he said. 'Why you make me find out for you what I find out, an' now you don't want to come? Tell me straight if you comin' or if you ain't, 'cause I can go long by myself.'

The woman looked up and frowned again. She held her glance this time as though she wanted us to be aware of her annoyance. She couldn't stand this disrespectful babbling in the presence of God, and God was present; for they had always said that wherever the two or three are gathered together in his name there He was also. She was still looking at us. Suddenly she turned her head and whispered something about respect for the word of God. The neighbour turned to another and whispered what the woman had said. The complaint was passed on to another three or four. They looked up and stared altogether as the first woman had done. The man who stood beside Boy Blue realized what was happening and so did those who stood nearest to me and Trumper. The woman seemed to want others, the saved and unsaved alike, to understand how she felt, and quite often the unsaved shared this kind of annoyance. We were gradually becoming as much a spectacle as the small boy and the preacher. We looked at each other and decided that we would go. And we didn't want anyone to understand why we were going. The women had dropped their heads.

'One by one,' Boy Blue said, 'an' I goin' first. Then you come all together.' We pretended not to hear or notice that Boy Blue had forced his way through. Trumper and I went on watching the preacher and the boy kneeling beside the table. They were praying in silence, and now the boy in the light looked terribly scared. The preacher was moved by his submission. The women looked up and seemed a little more at ease when they noticed that Boy Blue had gone. They had a feeling that he was what they would call the ring-leader. It was he who was prompting us in this disrespect. Trumper elbowed me again and made a sign with his head. The man beside him moved back and Trumper walked away. The man had understood what was happening and he seemed to keep the space clear expecting that I would leave at any moment. The women looked up, and it was clear that only one of us was left. They were sure that the first boy was the devil's one. It was Boy Blue who had brought us to mock the word of God and when this proved more than we could do he decided to take us away. They whispered among themselves in a kind of quiet indignation. Soon everything was quiet. The preacher had got up and was standing over the boy. I didn't know what would happen, but I had always heard them talk about sacrifice. I didn't know the meaning of sacrifice and I told myself that it was sacrifice which would follow. I was sure they were going to sacrifice him, and I wanted to see how it was done. The women looked across at me and the preacher saw them. He didn't seem to understand why they looked at me as they did. They dropped their heads and suddenly looked across again. The preacher turned away from the boy and made towards me. His face held the same stark uncalculating purpose I had noticed when he persuaded the boy to be saved. My thinking had become confused and for a moment I thought only of escaping that face and joining Trumper and Boy Blue. He made towards me with hands clasped and his head held up. I took a step back, saw him approach, turned and fought a way through the crowd. There was a flutter of giggles from the spectators. I heard the laughter. It became more and more distinct like the noise in a concert hall. I looked around for Trumper and Boy Blue hoping in the meantime to hear what the preacher would say. I heard a man say that if he wasn't careful he would lose the soul which he had fought so hard to win, and the laughter increased. Then there was a noise which seemed to be the preacher's voice, and soon the voices of the worshippers rose above the laughter and everything was under control. I walked away to join Trumper and Boy Blue as the voices carolled their testimony to my heart:

A ruler once came to Jesus by night
To ask him the way of salvation and light.
The Master replied in words clear and plain
You must be born again.

You must be born again,
You must be born again,
Verily, verily I say unto you,
You must be born again.

But for the street lamps where the roads crossed there was

no light. The glimmer of the candle had got lost within the thick circle of worshippers and spectators, yet I thought I could see the preacher's face standing out like a rock in the darkness and we could still hear the hymn about the ruler who went to Jesus by night. We hadn't spoken much since we met. Trumper seemed a bit angry that I should have stayed so long. He thought I shouldn't have cared about the women whispering among themselves or the way they looked at us. We walked very quietly between the trees over the weed, and I had a feeling we were thinking about the same thing. This wasn't the first time we had met together at an open-air meeting, although it was the first time we were going to do what Trumper had suggested. The words of the hymn seemed to fall like a fine drizzle through the trees and into our ears. You must be born again. You must be born again. There was something very frightening about them, and particularly the context in which they were placed. The hymn had been started in order to control the tittering of the spectators, and also perhaps because I had fled. It was as though one were reminded of an outstanding debt. The preacher was a kind of spiritual bailiff who offered salvation as a generous exchange for the other's suffering. You must be born again. You must be born again. They seemed to pursue us, and it wasn't clear whether we were still hearing the voices, but the words were there. You must be born again.

Cricket

Edward Brathwaite

Edward Brathwaite's contribution is nearer to prose-poetry than it is to the conventional short story; in fact, it is an anecdote which sharply illustrates the persuasiveness and the endemic poetry of one type of West Indian vernacular humour. It is also an accurate report in monologue of an incident in the recent history of West Indian cricket.

'Many a time I have seen him savin' the side,' the tailor was saying, as he sat and sewed in his shop. 'You remember that tourney wid Brandon? What-he-name now . . . that big-able water policeman . . . de one in charge o' the Harbour Patrol . . .'

'You mean Hop-a-long Cass? Is because a cow give he mother a kick before he did born that he foot come out so.'

'I know. But is not what I talkin' about. Ol' Hoppy was bowlin' that day as if he was Hurricane father. Lambert went in, playin' he know all about it as us'al, as *swoosh!* There he go fannin' outside the off-stump an' is *click!* He snick de ball straight in de slips.

' "Well boys, it look like we lossin' this match," says the skipper, writin' nought in the exercise book he was keepin' the score in. "You t'ink we could chance it an' sen' Gullstone in now before Charlie or Spooks?"

' "Yes, man," we all say.

'So Gullstone went in. You could see he face whitenin' under he skin an' you know that that saga-boy frighten : bat tappin', feet walkin' 'bout like they talkin' wid ants. Make it look like he never play cricket pun Brown's Beach before.

'But I've told him over an' over agen: *watch dé ball, man, watch de ball like it hook to you eye when you first goes in an' you don't know de pitch.* Uh doan mean to *poke;* but you jes' got to watch what you doin'. This isn't no time for playin' the fool or makin' no sport. This is cricket!

'But Gullstone too deaf. Mudder doan clean-out de wax in 'e ear!

'Firs' ball from Cass an' he fishin'.

'Secon' ball an' he missin'; swishin' he bat like he wishin' to catch butterfly, though de all Gullstone ever catch pun dis beach is a cold!

'But is always the trouble wid we: we too 'fraid an' too frighten. Is all very well when it rosy an' sweet; but let murder start an' *bruggalungdung*: you can't find a man to hold up de side.

'Look wha' happen las' week at de Oval!'

'At de Oval? Wha' happen las' week at de Oval?'

'You mean to say that you come in here wid that lime-skin cone you callin' a hat pon you head, an' them slip slop shoe strap on to you foot like a touris'; you sprawlin' you ass all over muh chair widdout askin' please leave nor licence; wastin' my time when you know very well that I can't find enough to finish these zoot suits 'fore is Christmas; an' on top o' all this, you could find enough nerve to stop me cool cool cool in de middle o' all my needle an' t'read; make me prick me hand in me haste; an' tell me broad an' bold to muh face THAT YOU DOAN REALLY KNOW WHAT HAPPEN AT KENSINGTON OVAL?

'We was ONLY playin' de MCC, man. . . .'

'M . . . C . . . C . . . ?'

'Who come all de way out from Ingland!

'We was battin' you see; score wasn't too bad: one hundred an' ninety-seven for three. The openers out; Tae Worrell out; Everton Weekes just glide two for fifty, an' now the GIANT to come!

'Feller name Wardle was bowlin': tossin' up sweet sweet sweet slow-medium syrup.

'Firs' ball . . . "N . . . o . . . o . . ."

'Back down de wicket to Wardle.

'Secon' ball . . . "N . . . o . . . o . . . o . . ."

'Back down de wicket to Wardle.

'Third ball comin' up an' ev'rybody know what goin' happen. . . .

'*Clap clap clap clap*; we all watchin' Clyde as we clap Wardle up to de wicket, an' *prax!*[1]

'Clyde back pun he back foot, through extra-cover, an' is four red runs all de way!

'"You see dat shot?" the people was shoutin'. "Jesus Christ, man, you see dat shot?"

'All over de ground you could see fellers shakin' hands wid each other as if it was they who was makin' de strokes; as if it was them had the power. One man run out pun de field wid a red fowl-cock goin' quawk quawk in he han' an' would'a give it to Clyde right then an' there, I suppose, if de police didn't stop he!

'An' in front o' where I was sittin', one bald-headed man snatch off he hat as if he was crazy an' pointin' he finger at

---

[1] *prax!* – The sound of the bat striking the ball; an example of *Onomatopoeia*, which· is the formation of names or words from sounds that resemble those associated with the object or the action to be named.

Wardle, he jump up an' down like a jack-in-de-box shoutin'
out: "Blood . . . big . . . boy . . . bring . . . me . . . he
. . . blood . . . !"

'Who would'a think that for twenty-five years he was
standin' up in them Post Office cages sellin' de Gover'ment
stamps! If I wasn't there to see fuh myself, I would'a never
believe it.

'But uh say it once an' uh say it agen: When things goin'
good, you cahn touch we. But let murder start? An' you
can't find a man to hol' up the side.

'Like when they decide to bring Laker on. . . . Goin'
remember what happenin' then for as long as I live. . . .

'This Laker a tall, quiet, heavy-face fellow who before he
start to do anything is hitch up he pants round he belly. He
bowlin' off-breaks.

'He stroll up slow to de wicket. He int make no fuss; jus'
toss up de firs' one an' *bap!* Clyde play forward firm an' de
ball hit he pad an' fly up over de wicket.

'Laker hitch up he pants an' toss up de secon'. It pitchin'
off-stump an' comin' back sharp.

'Clyde stretch right out like a man in de dark an' he kill it.
'"N . . . o . . . o . . . o . . . o . . . o . . . ," cry de
schoolboys

'Then this Laker come down wid 'e third. He wrap up
de ball in he han' like a package AN' MAKE CLYDE WALCOTT
LOOK FOOLISH!

'Mister man, you could hear all de flies that was buzzin'
out there round de bread carts in de silence that suck in it
breath at de Oval. The ball itself pop up in de air as if it,
too, was surprise.

'"Watch it, man, Clyde," was all we could say when we
settle back down from surprise.

'BUT IT HAPPEN AGAIN! De very same way! An' this is uh man who could hit a fas' bowler fuh six off he back foot, yuh know!

'So as soon as Laker see this, he hitch up he pants an' call three men to creep up close to de wicket. They stop up there wid their hands out like claws, they eyes pushin' out o' they heads like is crabs.

'"Kill one o' dem, Clyde," somebody was shoutin'. "Knock they skull off! Doan let them tangle you up in no leg trap! Use de feet dat God give yuh!"

'Ev'ry blabber-mout' talkin'. Ev'rybody givin' advice. But we so frighten now at what happenin' there, we could all wet we pants if we don't have a care.

'An' Jim Laker comin' agen.

'"Swing de bat, man!" one feller shout out an' Clyde Walcott swing but de bat miss de ball an' de ball hit he pad an' he pad went *biff* wid de whole o' de MCC side in de air wid a loud HOWZATT like they want to fight an' when we look back de umpire hand stick up stiff stiff stiff like a man who dead an' de best o' we batsmen out.

'The crowd so surprise they int sayin' a thing. Ev'ry mout' loss.

'But when Lucas come in they start up agen, loadin' de place wid advice: Watch dis. Watch dat. Hit he hard, man. Hit he hard. He int bowlin' nutten. Knock he to hell off he length. Tip an' run an' let Everton take a turn in 'e ass. . . .

'But Lucas lookin' so cheerful an' laughin' an' wavin' he bat as he spring-steppin' out to de wicket, that we think after all that de man is a fluke when is *plix!* Johnny Lucas off-stump cock back in de air like a lorry gear-stick in reverse.

E

'Boy! Then you should hear how de people get on!

'"No-ball!" they all shoutin'. "You int see de man peltin'! Umpire! You int see de man peltin'!"

'"See! How you t'ink he goin' see it! You int see that the umpire buy out a'ready! You t'ink that the MCC come over here, all de way from they Lords an' Buckin'ham Palace where I hear they got de Ashes hide 'way; you think they gwine come all de way over here an' let some poor-tail small-islander side throw stick in de pooch o' de very game they invent?"

'"*Who* invent it, you say?

'"An' *who* de hell, by de way, you is callin' a small-island side?"

'"Awright! Awright! But de umpire buy-out, I tell you! If they cahn win by fair means, they got to win we by foul.

'"Boogles, boy!"

'Boogles Williams come out.

'"Boogles, boy! Doan let them get de Hat Trick!"

'Is all de crowd worry an' bodder 'bout now: not to let Laker get de Hat Trick.

'"Boogles, boy! Doan let them get de Hat Trick!"

'But uh say it once an' uh say it agen: tha' is always the way wid we people. When things goin' good, you cahn touch we. But let murder start; an' ol' man, you can't find a man to hold up de side. . . .

'Excep' Bebe. Many a time I have seen him savin' the side,' said the tailor, as he sat and sewed in his shop. 'You remember that tourney wid Brandon . . . ?'

Bebe pushed the three whitewood sticks all together into the sand until he, who was six feet tall, was twice as

tall as they were. Then he made eleven straight ships in
the sand as he walked down the pitch and pushed a fourth
stick in the sand where he stopped. And while the boys
threw the ball like a white-bird flash from Gullstone to
Tailor to Tonic to Bree, with a click as each caught it clean
in his hand like a bird in a cage, Bebe ("Run yuh captain –
firs'-pick," he would shout) walked away from the wicket
and dipped his bat in the sea.

All the best players went and dipped their bats in the sea.
If you were small or couldn't bat well, you couldn't dip
your bat in the sea.

But Bebe and Lambert and Tonic and Bree always dipped
their bats in the sea: up past their ankles in lappity water,
tip-toeing if the water was cold, they would lean to the water
and slap it three times with the bat of the wood of the
clamma-cherry² tree. Slap wood on water. Dip it. Walk
back. Leaving a trail in the water. This was for luck, a
prayer for power, and a special mark of prestige.

So Bebe slapped water, dipping his bat three times in the
sea, and stood, for a moment, the tide's silver chains round
his ankles; then turned, the sun's ball flashing full from his
bat as he turned, dragging the delicate chains of the water
as far up the beach as they'd go as he walked slowly up to
the wicket.

---

² *clamma-cherry* – A starchy-sweet, cloudy-white West Indian cherry. It
is called the *clamma cherry* in Jamaica because of its 'clammy' (moist and
sticky) taste. In Guyana it is boiled into a thick paste and used as a sealing-
gum in kite-making.

The Reckoning

Jan Carew

Jan Carew's 'The Reckoning', an extract made by the author from his first novel, Black Midas, *is an exciting Guyanese adventure tale which demonstrates the qualities of courage, selflessness and integrity side by side with the everyday human weaknesses of cowardice, envy and greed.*

Three of us set out from Perenong in pursuit of Santos and my uncle Richard Smart. These two were trying to escape across the Cuyuni backlands with a sack of diamonds which they had stolen from Bullah Daniel's shop on the waterfront. They had had twelve hours start, but Tonic, although he had been wounded in a brawl a few nights before and his head was bandaged, he was certain that we could overtake the thieves before they reached Nameless River.

We walked around the hill and forded the Perenong Creek above Grass Fall. The sun was bending towards its four o'clock mooring, sparkling high above us in the tree tops. In the half-dark, half-light of the forest, strands of greenheart and mora surrounded us. The earth was as red as canna lilies, and as we walked along the winding trail we occasionally came across bright patches where fallen trees had let in the sunlight. Butterflies with incandescent wings hung like small lanterns in the twilight. The forest darkened and in many places the trail was overgrown. The red earth changed to white and then brown sand. Tonic walked with

68

quick shuffling steps like an Indian. We passed growths of wild pineapple and giant azaleas. I only knew that it was night when I looked up and saw a star through a hole in the roof of leaves. We walked one pace apart, so close that I could not tell if the noises that walked with us were the sound of the wind, our breathing or the soft crunch of our footsteps in the sand.

'This is snake country,' Tonic said and the darkness boxed up his voice so that only we could hear it.

'It must feel just like this walking under a river,' I thought. 'The darkness has weight; it sits on top of us, and every time we part it, throw it aside, it closes in behind us.'

Red howlers[1] broke the long silence, and as if the whole forest was waiting for a signal, tinamous[2] and saki-winkies[3] joined in.

'How you feeling, boy?' Bullah Daniels asked Tonic.

'All right, skipper.'

'Tell me if the head giving you trouble, 'cause when we reach the hill country it's going to be rough, boy.'

'The head feels fine, skipper.'

I thought about Santos and my uncle. I had to think about something real, for the forest was too full of melancholy noises.

'I can feel the thoughts ticking round your head, Shark,' Bullah said. 'You worried 'bout the diamonds, eh?'

'Not the diamonds so much, Bullah; somehow I feel better about that part of it. I don't mind if I've got to start

---

[1] *red howlers* – Noisy Guyanese baboons with large chin-pouches which amplify their slightest utterance.

[2] *tinamous* – Quail-like game-birds, with a high-pitched fluting voice, found in Guyana and throughout South America.

[3] *saki-winkies* – Small, squint-eyed Guyanese monkeys.

all over again; I know you will stake me enough to make a fresh beginning.'

'Well, it's what, then?'

'It's that Uncle Richard of mine, Bullah; I don't care what you and Tonic say, I know that looking for those two is like trying to find a sand-fly in a bush. Richard is the brain behind Santos; he's like a tree-lizard; he can take on any colour or shape. He's a devil I tell you, Bullah, a real devil.'

'But you tell me your grandma put a curse on him; and pardner, old people curse bad like a sword. We will catch up with them, Shark; mark my words.'

We were still on the move at day-clean.[4] The forest was thinning out and sunlight hung from trees to earth like luminous mosquito nets.

'We should hit the swamp any time now,' Tonic said and his voice sounded heavy. Bullah must have noticed too because he said, 'We can take a rest when we reach the swamp.'

We stopped at the edge of the swamp and put our packs down. Tonic stretched out on the sand and closed his eyes. I had been carrying my balata pouch so long that even when I put it down I kept leaning forward as if the weight was still on my back. I washed and dressed Tonic's wound while Bullah stood over us anxiously. Tonic fell asleep moaning softly and Bullah and I walked away.

'You think the boy can make it?' Bullah asked.

'I don't know. Tonic won't say how he really feels; he'd rather drop dead than admit he can't go on.'

---

[4] *day-clean* – A poetic expression (and an everyday description) of the dawn in Guyana. *Fore-day mornin'* in Trinidad, and *Sun up* or *Early o'clock* in Jamaica.

'That boy means a lot to me, Shark; I rather lose everything I got than sacrifice him. Fifteen years since he's been with me. Look, Shark, if bad comes to the worse you will have to push on alone.'

Tonic woke up when the sun was high and a haze sizzled over the swamp water and the hills. I was fighting against sleep and my eyes felt as if they had dust in them. Tonic made a great show of feeling better, but his eyes were glazed and when he stood up his hands hung down as if they were weighted. We crossed the first stretch of sand and reached the hills. Tonic picked up the trail of the two men but we veered off to the left, away from it. From the top of the first hill we saw giant trees in the valley below us, amaratas, moras, kakaralis where bright-plumaged birds flashed across shafts of light.

Beside the dead, silent swamp on our right, the trees seemed to live and breathe. We had been following a winding trail, and the sun shone from contrary directions as we walked on. Towards noon we came to another stretch of swamp. The sun was directly overhead and the heat pelted down, stinging, scorching, pricking my skin with tiny thorns of fire. We threaded our way carefully, avoiding fallen trees and looking out for snakes. Flies rose up and stung our eyeballs until we were almost blinded. We reached the wooded hills on the other side of the swamp. It was dark under the trees, and I felt that we were not alone, that all around eyes were watching our progress. Bullah grew restless and, as if he had expected us to catch up with our enemies, he climbed high into a greenheart and scanned the country around. The hills rose gradually and tumbled down steeply, making the descent harder than the climb.

We stopped to prepare tea and Tonic sat with his back against a tree trunk.

'The boy don't look too good,' Bullah said and I noticed that Tonic's bandage was stained with blood. I changed it and washed the wound with lysol. Tonic clenched his teeth so hard that I could see the bulge of muscle by the curve of his jaw and I could feel his temples pounding.

'How's it, boy?' I asked.

'Drums,' he said, 'drums inside me head.' And he slumped over in a faint. He came-to quickly, willing himself better. 'Jus' feel a little bit tired,' he whispered.

'We staying here,' Bullah said.

'Is all right, skipper, is all right I tell you.' He stood up with an effort and braced himself against a tree.

'Tell Shark the way; we stopping here till you feel better!' Bullah said.

'I swear I can make it, skipper; it's about four hours' walk from here to Nameless River, straight as a die across those hills.' Bullah lifted him gently and lay him on the sand.

'Leave the bandage with me, Shark, and any food you can spare. I want to go on but it's this boy or the diamonds. I will wait for you for two days and if you don't come I will head back and put the police on those two thieves' tail if I got to go all the way to Bartica.'

I understood that Bullah was saying goodbye and I felt angry with him because everything he said or implied was true. He could strip away the fantasy and expose the core even when it was a matter of life and death. Silence settled over us. I was annoyed with Tonic that he should have fallen sick, angry with Bullah because in a moment of crisis he had discovered that in my greed I would sacrifice the life of a friend for a sack of diamonds.

'Don't take it to heart, Shark, life's got plenty lessons to teach you yet, pardner; this bush does reduce you to an animal and then you got to fight your way back to prove you are a man. You better get moving, and don't make sundown catch you before you reach Nameless River.'

I left half of my supplies with Bullah and Tonic, poured boiling water into the barrel of my rifle, tested the action of the bolt and set out. I knew Bullah and Tonic were watching me but I didn't look back. I walked quickly, feeling my prospecting knife slapping against my thigh. The forest darkened, and my footsteps sounded loud under the tall trees. I wasn't afraid of animals or snakes, and for the first time, I felt certain that I would overtake my uncle and Santos. The only fear I knew was for the thing I was about to do with no witness but God and the forest trees.

But this fear was remote as I swung downhill. The sense of being alone filled me with a particular gladness. I looked up at the sun and quickened my pace. I saw Nameless River from a hill top. The molasses-black stream flowed by a hundred yards away. For a long time I stood still watching every movement below and scanning the far bank of the river. I descended stealthily until I came to a mora tree which leaned over the river. I hid my balata pouch between the roots and crouched down to wait.

When Santos and Uncle Richard appeared from behind the hill they looked small and tired and their clothes were torn in several places, probably by thorns. They each carried a shotgun and a large pack.

'That was a brute walk,' Santos said as they passed me not ten yards away.

''Cross the river is open country; we safe boy!' Richard said. He was taller and leaner than his companion and the sunlight gleamed on his dark demonic handsome face. I did not wait for them to unharness their packs.

'Richard!' I called out, holding the rifle steady. They spun round.

'Oh, is that you, boy,' Richard said.

'Don't touch your guns or move!' I shouted. I saw Richard's eyes gleam and he smiled. His teeth were so white it looked as if he had electric bulbs in his mouth.

'Where you' friends, nephew?' he asked.

'I just want to have a few words with the two of you; listen to me carefully and don't make a wrong move. Throw your guns down, well away from you and then throw the diamonds; I know you've got them around your waists. Move on!'

I fired a shot so that it kicked up sand between them. I rammed another cartridge into the breach. Santos was frightened but Richard was still smiling. Santos obeyed but his partner hesitated.

'You got to come and get the diamonds yourself, boy,' Richard said. Suddenly he threw his pack down and ran for the river. I fired at his right thigh and the force of the bullet staggered him momentarily. He gained the river and swam strongly for the opposite bank. I wavered. I hated my uncle but I did not want to kill him. We heard a shout and the dark water around the swimmer was turned into white froth.

'The perai[5] got him!' Santos shouted in a hoarse voice. The cannibal fish bit and spun away and returned to the

---

[5] *perai* – *Piraya* or *piranha*; one of the most vicious varieties of freshwater fish.

attack. I felt as if a cold iron shaft had been driven through my spine. I had words on the tip of my tongue but could not utter them.

'You murder him! You murder him! Oh, God!' Santos said, covering his eyes and sobbing. Soon all was quiet and the mora tree leaned over to gaze at a rippleless shadow.

'The old lady's curse came true on Nameless River,' I found myself saying, 'and the curse has caught up with Richard Smart.'

I turned away from the river. I was anxious to get away. I knew that my uncle's devil's soul would haunt this place forever, emerge from the black ooze to cry out up and down the banks as soon as darkness fell.

'Come on!' I said to Santos. 'You carry the dead man's pack; we've got a long night's march.' His eyes were fixed on the river, staring, staring. 'Come on!' I shouted. And he got up and walked ahead of me very meekly.

Tacama

Edgar Mittelholzer

*'Tacama' is the odd-story-out in the anthology in that it is
the only one in which the author has depicted a landscape,
a section of a setting, with the same descriptive care and
penetrating insight given to the portrayal of a human
character in another kind of narrative tale. In other words,
in 'Tacama' a physical background is raised to the level of
a central character and is given fictional heroic status. The
story is set in Guyana and Edgar Mittelholzer attempts to
give the jungle setting a unique presence which is not unlike
the aura of a spine-chilling ghost story.*

Tacama is straggly and of a desultory nature.

When the *corial*[1] drew up by the bank that February day,
I stepped ashore and told Charles that I wanted to do a bit
of exploring.

'This spot rather takes my fancy,' I said.

He waved me off.

'Not coming with me then?'

'No, thanks. I'll stay just here and laze. A holiday was
made for lazing – not to go tramping about in the hot sun
asking for sun-stroke.'

'I won't be five minutes,' I told him.

He covered his head with a towel against the eye-flies and

---

[1] *corial* – The largest and most river-worthy of all the Guyanese Indian
flat-bottomed river boats.

stretched out under a wild cacao tree by the water's edge.

'See and keep to the track, Peter!' he called after me, lifting the towel an instant.

'My sense of direction is excellent,' I assured him, as I began to plod up the sand. 'I won't get lost, if that's what you mean.'

The track that leads past the corrals[2] is clearly defined. Out of curiosity, I followed it until it came to a point where I could see it snaking without interruption into the mirage-distance of the vast savannah that opens out to the west and south. I had no inclination to go any further along it. It was the jungle that interested me. I like jungles.

Imprinted indistinctly, but unmistakably, everywhere on the sand were the marks of beasts and men; no rain had fallen for weeks to wash them out.

A crooked tree to the left of the track attracted my attention. It was bare of leaves except at the very top, and appeared to be slowly dying from the drought. It looked like a young *mora*.[3] It seemed to grin greyly at me in its death-thirst; it seemed, as I watched it, to wilt visibly in the heat that rose from the sand.

I stood and observed the heat for a minute. It swirled around me like swathes of molten silk.

The tree caught my attention again. As I have said, a crooked tree. A tree, I thought, fatally enmeshed.

This thought gave me a mental pause. In this instant, it was as though an arresting tick had sounded in my brain. . . . Why fatally enmeshed? Enmeshed in what? Surf? . . . The

---

[2] *corrals* – Pens for horses or for cattle; or enclosures for capturing wild animals; also defensive encampments.

[3] *mora* – A very large rain-forest tree growing near rivers and streams.

wind makes a noise like surf in the tops of the trees.... You listen and hear it coming.... You mistake it for rain... But it is only the wind....

I shook myself and walked towards the tree. I felt the sun on my bare head. It might have been a brassy ghost sinisterly subjecting me to an unpleasant barbering.

Ants kept crawling up the thin, sap-dry trunk of the tree – a long cavalcade of large black ants. One of them paused and regarded me with enquiry – mayhap with warning. It seemed to make signals. Infinitesimal semaphore. The others left it behind for a moment. Then it went on abruptly, no doubt considering that it had given me far more attention than a mere specimen of *homo sapiens* deserved.

I watched them for a while. Hundreds, thousands, of black jungle ants. There are no ants like these on the coast.

I wondered about them. Ants were supposed to be intelligent creatures. Science has even hinted that they may communicate with each other by means of a definite language. Who could tell if these black ants did not keep a history of their race written on particles of leaves and stored underground in vaults known only to themselves? Could it not be that their ancestors had smiled cynically at some hapless Dutch planter of 1763 pursued and hacked to death by a party of slaves? Perhaps these ants possessed, in pin-point catacombs, lost beneath this white sand, more valuable records of the great slave insurrection than Rodway's *History of British Guiana*. One never knew about ants.

The whim took me to discover where they were coming from.

I noticed that they were moving from the sand up on to the trunk of the tree. Without disturbing the line, I edged away and traced it into a copse of swizzle-stick trees. I en-

tered the copse. It was not dense, and there was ample room
for movement. I was now in the jungle proper, but no
lianas[4] stretched across my path, as Hollywood might have
depicted it. No crocodiles slithered out of a swamp and
opened toothy jaws at me, nor did any evil, spotted snakes
uncoil themselves in readiness to strike. In fact, the silence
seemed to be the only threatening presence. It lived. It
swirled and groped at me, insinuated itself into my senses
with deliberate purpose. It allied itself to the sun and smothered me with unwelcome caresses. It watched me and
smiled secretly to itself.

I glanced back to make sure that I could still see the
crooked tree, deciding to keep it always in view, as a landmark, just in case, by chance, I did feel uncertain of my
bearings.

I followed the line of black ants further into the copse. I
trod on a dry leaf, and the sound rose like the cracking of
glass, and seemed to evoke from the silence a snarl as at a
sacrilege committed. It gave me a guilty feeling. I nearly
apologized. In future, I vowed, I would tread on no more
dry leaves.

I moved on.

The vegetation was low and still sparse; it afforded no
protection for my head. The ants led me to a clump of wild-
pines. The line turned off towards another copse of swizzle-
stick trees, but at this point I decided that the game was too
pointless and puerile. The sun was too hot; I must get out of
it and return to Charles. I could feel a dizziness which I
knew was not good. I rested my hand on my head; my head
felt baked.

[4] *lianas* – Decorative types of climbing and twining forest vines.

Before I could turn off, however, I caught sight of something white down the centre of the wild-pine clump. A wild-pine sends up long, pointed, tapering leaves – leaves hard and saw-edged. To fall into or against a clump of wild-pines can result in serious injury – ugly gashes and scratches. So I had to be careful how I leaned over and peered down into the core of this cluster.

I saw a milky-white web spun across the young leaves far down within the hollow of the cluster. There was a hole in this web – jumbie-dark[5] and mysterious. But there was no jumbie in this hole. Out of it protruded two hairy, blue-black legs, tipped with crimson.

I stood entranced – dizzy and entranced.

All spiders are my enemies – and here was a bush one. A large, hairy blue-black one.

A shudder crawled down my back – a shudder which my brain translated into blue-black hairy legs scurrying on my bare skin. I wriggled and slapped at my back. I laughed a low perverse laugh.

A new situation faced me now. I had to do something about it.

I stooped and picked up a twig. I smiled and trembled, but stretched out and dropped the twig deliberately down into the web.

It was a light twig, and when it landed on the web it stuck and hung.

Four blue-black, hairy legs sprang horribly out of the hole, and two fangs waited, poised and savagely expectant.

This was good – terrifying but good.

The scientists say that there are none of us without a streak

5 *jumbie-dark* – Ghost-infested darkness.

of masochism.[6] Well, this was the form mine took. I stood there for how long I don't know, dropping twigs down and teasing that spider and at the same time frightening myself to death.

Suddenly it occurred to me to glance up to make sure that the crooked tree was still in view.

It was not — and a hollow ache moved inside me. I stiffened and lost interest in the spider.

Something crackled behind me.

I started round.

Not a twig moved. Not a leaf. So I had to conclude it must have been the silence chuckling at me.

I turned round and round, thinking to catch it off-guard. But it was too clever.

A black lizard darted across the sand from one twig to another.

I heard the surf, far away, dying almost as it began.

I must look for the line of ants, I thought. It would be a simple matter to follow the line back to the crooked tree.

I looked — but there were no ants.

I turned round and round again, and smiled. I wanted to chuckle, as the silence had chuckled, but my chuckle would have sounded like thunder, and I wasn't in the mood to hear thunder.

I moved around a bit, then came back to the wild-pine cluster. I looked down into the web, but could not see the spider. It must have retreated deep down into the hole.

My twigs should have been there caught in the web. They weren't there.

---

[6] *a streak of masochism* — Some evidence in one's personality of a willingness to receive and accept pleasure from pain or humiliation inflicted on oneself.

This, I knew, was laughable. The spider wouldn't have pulled my twigs down into its web. A twig wasn't a fly. A spider couldn't say to a twig: 'Come into my parlour.'

It must be a different wild-pine cluster. I must have wandered off from the original one. This was a new one.

It began to shake inside me – a brown sponge. My mouth felt dry.

I clasped my hands together and rested them on my head. My head felt like a hot-plate with the current not too long ago switched off. When I pressed on it I found that I wanted to stagger. For a moment I did stagger. And the wild-pine leaves reached at me. I had to dodge to evade them. They were blue-black and hairy, and tipped with crimson.

I nearly whimpered, but knew that it would be fatal to show fright in sound as well as in mime. I always had to reckon with the silence.

Somehow, I managed to steady myself. I sat down and felt something solid come up to meet me. I looked down and saw that it was the trunk of a fallen palm. I had no idea where the trunk of a fallen palm could have appeared from, but I wouldn't let this new topic corrode my *morale*. It was job enough dealing with the heat and the silence.

I sat very still and tried to concentrate, tried to stop the heat from wrapping me round with too much molten silk. There were yards and yards of it all round me. An endless winding-sheet.

Not a good thought that last one. Winding – sheet.

I made no move; I would not answer. I looked down and thought I would have seen white sand, but there was a carpet of leaves – soft and damp. Leaves that must have been piling up since the time of Governor van Hoogenheim. I noticed that the shadows had a strange shape. They oughtn't to have been so long as they were. When I had left Charles it was noon. That was a few minutes ago, so why did the shadows look so elongated? At noon shadows are short: dwarves that move under you so that you can stamp on them and keep them in subjection. It's only when they grow tall behind you in the afternoon that they get out of control and follow you round with evil intent.

I looked up.

The sun was more than half-way down to the horizon in the west.

I heard the voice calling me again. It sounded so much like Charles's voice that I rose and moved towards where I fancied it came from.

I went on moving towards it, and it called louder.

Then I saw the crooked tree; I moved round a cluster of wild-pines, round a clump of swizzle-stick trees – and there I was back on the track. And there was Charles coming towards me shouting my name.

He said that he had fallen into a doze and awakened at half-past three, and had seen no sign of me. 'You gave me a fright, man. Did you get lost or what?'

I told him not to be an ass. Of course I hadn't got lost.

I laughed. 'See that crooked tree there? I kept it as my landmark. How could I get lost with a tree like that for landmark?'

I laughed again. 'It was just the heat that delayed me a bit, Charles. And the silence. Wicked. Tried to wrap me in a winding-sheet.'

He gave me a funny look, caught my arm, hurried me to the water's edge and began to bathe my head.

Hurricane

John Hearne

'Hurricane' is yet another extract from a very interesting novel. It has been edited from John Hearne's third book The Faces of Love, *and named by the editor in agreement with the author. As its title suggests the story has a very strong dramatic and narrative appeal. It is economically written at a quick pace, and the sense of tragedy with which it ends highlights the traditional struggle of man with the forces of nature.*

We were more than half-way down to the Pen before I told them that we ought to stop. We had come down from the Gap very fast, with Ferdie riding behind each of us in turn. This was late in the afternoon, almost dark. The sky was streaky and brown; it had become grubbier with every hour that we rode. The air felt as if you were being stuffed under hot blankets and the leaves were absolutely still. When you listened it felt strange, and you realized this was because you weren't hearing any insects but only the water down the hillsides. The dogs were ahead. They ran swiftly, with their heads low, and they didn't snap among themselves.

'We'll have to stop here,' I said loudly and pulled on the reins.

'No,' Carl said. 'Let's go on. It'll be less to cover back to the Pen afterwards.' His big face was pinched and tight with anxiety.

'If we don't stop here,' I said, 'we'll get caught in the valley and be washed away for sure.'

'Listen to him, Mass' Carl,' John Graham said. 'Him know what him say.' He had turned his mule across the little trail.

Jojo and Oliver didn't say anything. Carl looked at them and they nodded to Graham and me.

'Turn the beasts loose,' I said, 'and let's dig in. Hurry, eh. We don't have much time.' We were high up on the shoulder of a hill. It was grassy and smooth and there was another hill behind us that would break the full wind. There was nowhere else we could go. When we got down from the mules and began to dig a shelf out of the hillside with the machetes, the beasts wouldn't move. They stayed close, and the dogs lay flat along the ground and never took their eyes from us.

We dug a narrow shelf into the hillside. It was like a trench except that the sides were one above the other. The ground sloped before us down to a river. There was a large grove of trees behind us on the left. When we all got into the trench with the dogs it was unbearably hot. The mules stayed near. We had taken the rifles and shot-guns from them, and the three bottles of rum. There wasn't room for anything else in the trench. I didn't think we would have to wait long. While we were waiting I scrambled out and went to my mule and took my plastic wash-bag from the saddle-bag. I emptied what it held back into the saddle-bag and put my cigarettes into the waterproof plastic. I went back into the trench and held the bag open for the other packets of cigarettes. The mule tried to push its head into the trench and we had to slap the coarse, bony face before it would go away. We were all listening and watching the still leaves on the trees across the river. It was almost night and we could just see the leaf spray of the branches.

'Here it is,' I said and watched the branches dip and shiver and the long grass ruffle. It was bent delicately for half a second and then went flat and ugly as the wind leapt over the hill with a solid, roaring scream. The rain came before the wind; a scatter of big drops first, and then a thick almost horizontal wall of grey. Just before the water shuttered everything from sight, we saw a big cinchona[1] bounce madly, root over branch, down the hillside. The hill was quivering like a big animal and one of the dogs had its head inside my shirt. For about five minutes after the rain there was a peculiar light, half-grey, half-luminous. Then it was dark. It was too dark to see anything at all; and the only sounds were the screaming, steady bellow of the wind and the pounding of the rain on the hillside. The trench was wet and it had become suddenly cool. I was between Oliver and Ferdie.

It went on for five hours. At first it didn't seem possible that the wind could keep to that unrelaxing, unvarying shriek. But it did. We were very cold and the floor of the little dug-out was muddy and chill. Water as it ran down the hillside poured in a sheet across the entrance of the dug-out. The wind and the rain were too loud for us to distinguish other noises plainly, but sometimes there was the deep clang of thunder coming through the sound they made. Sometimes, too, there was a confused ripping crash. When my teeth began to chatter, I took the bottle of rum from inside my shirt and passed it to Ferdie beside me. He drank and gave the bottle to his father. After Carl had taken some they passed it back to me and I handed it to Oliver for him and Jojo. I was glad when it was my turn. The spirit caught

---

[1] *cinchona* – A large shade tree; an evergreen yielding the cinchona bark from which quinine and other drugs are derived.

keenly in my throat and the glow of its heat began before it was in my stomach.

Then the wind began to lull. It was still strong, but without that high deadly scream, and we could hear the fast, deep roar of the river below us. The rain still drove loudly before the wind. I felt Jojo shake me hard, reaching across Oliver to do it.

'Come here!' he bawled. I could hardly catch the words, even in the little box we had dug. He sounded serious.

I crawled over Oliver, squeezing between him and the earth above. Jojo took my hand and thrust it into the darkness outside. The water pouring across the entrance was cold and the driven rain stung my flesh.

'Feel that!' he bellowed close in my ear and pushed my hand into a very fast rush of water. I felt around outside the entrance and up the hillside behind our trench, as far as my arm would go. All I could feel was the deep, thick race of water. Jojo shone his torch beside me and I saw the rain in the beam and then the crumpled, shiny surface of the water where a new channel had been scooped into the hillside. The water was very fast and it was coming down the hill just beside our trench and across the slope before the entrance. There was only a narrow strip of safe land left, over on Carl's side. The surface of the water was very near to the entrance and when I plunged my arm in, I couldn't touch the bottom.

'Let's get out of here!' I shouted to Jojo. I was very frightened and wondered how long we had before the gully race² washed our dug-out into the river. He nodded, and I crawled back quickly and shouted the facts to Graham and Carl.

² *gully race* – A very rapid stream of water running along the course of a gully.

'Mind the wind doesn't blow you in!' I yelled as Carl began to crawl out of the trench. In the torch-beam I could see him pressed flat and digging his fingers into the ground as he wriggled out and up. The low bank of the channel looked very near. Graham and Ferdie went next. The man crawled with his body between the wind and his son; the boy had one arm tight round his father's neck and his free arm thrust sideways and stiff, the fingers dug into the earth. Carl helped them up beside him. I put the torch back into my pocket and poked my head out. The wind caught me and I began to skid helplessly, tumbling sideways towards the water. I sank my fingers up to their knuckles in the rain-soft ground and pressed into the mud. Then I felt Graham's enormous hand close on my wrist, and the light from Carl's torch shone in my face. There was a noise between howling and hissing in the night around me. As I scrambled up beside the other two, a huge rain-drop hurtling on the wind, hit me in the eyeball. It hurt like the stone from a catapult. Lying flat on the hillside above the tumbling water in the new gully was not hard. The wind kept pushing under us but it was safe enough. I joined my torch to Carl's, and in the grey, packed lines of rain I saw Oliver's head and shoulders come out from the trench. The wind rolled him as he came out and Graham reached down and grabbed his wrist. Between them they began to drag him up beside us. I was shining my light on the wrist Graham held and I could see Oliver's thin small hand sprouting from the other man's huge, flat one. Then I saw the hand vanishing into the first and felt Graham lunge forward beside me and lifting the beam up I caught Oliver's white face among the rain as the wind hit him square and pushed him into the darkness where the gully was. I saw this, and in the same instant heard Jojo's bellow of, 'Oliver!' burst through the howling wind; and saw the quick blur of his body against the rain-dimmed beam of the torch as he dived from the dug-out into the water.

Carl, Graham, Ferdie and I spent the rest of the night up the hillside, under the grove of trees. None of them had blown down and with the wind dropping it was the safest place to be until daylight. We had left the dogs to follow if they could, but they hadn't come after us as we crawled up the hill in the mud and flattened grass. I had no feeling inside me, except a numb disbelief. The two bodies going into the water seemed like so many years ago; in another country.

The Visitor

H. Orlando Patterson

H. Orlando Patterson is one of the most engaging of the 'new wave' of West Indian novelists to have been published within the last few years. Like his first novel, The Children of Sisyphus, *this short story is about one of the pressing social problems in Jamaica; but 'The Visitor' is not a sociologist's excuse to write a fictionalized report: it is, indeed, a compassionate writer's way of making his readers become socially aware. Hardly a full-length short story, it is more an incident in cameo.*

He was odd. Below his grey, felt hat he had an uncertain smile which confused me a little as I somehow got the strange impression that I was making him uncomfortable. He remained silent for a long time. I began to detect something sinister about him.

Suddenly, he said, in an almost apologetic voice, 'You Miss Gladys's son?' There was a faint smell of rum and toothpaste. I nodded. He kept staring at me; his mouth remained slightly open. His eyes were watery, curious and a little sad.

'You want me to call her for you?' I asked.

'What?' He seemed surprised that I was capable of asking a question; or perhaps that I had been daring enough to put one to him. He swallowed, stared at me with even greater curiosity, and then murmured, 'Oh, call her? Yes, yes, do that.'

90

What a funny man, I thought, as I went to the door.

'Mamma.'

'What?'

'A man out here to see you.'

'A man? Which man that?'

'Don't know him. Never seen him before.'

She got up and peeped through the window. By now I was anxious myself to know who the stranger might be and so I observed her closely as she peered outside at him. She stared and stared. She did not move and seemed petrified by the window. I walked inside and had a mild shock as I saw her expression.

'What happen, Mamma?'

She did not answer. I realized that something was very wrong. I had never known her to be confronted with a situation which she seemed in any way incapable of handling. Not until that moment.

'Mamma . . . ?'

'Go an' tell 'im me not here . . . go an' tell 'im . . . no, wait, tell 'im . . . tell 'im me coming.'

Whoever the stranger was I realized that he somehow threatened us and instinctively began to fear him. Yet, when I walked back to him his appearance instilled little apprehension in me. His manner was uncertain, vague and distant. It reassured me against my every instinct. I even had, for a moment, the absurd impression that he was afraid of us. And this flattered my childhood pride.

'My mother says she coming,' I told him.

He said thanks softly. My mother walked out of the door, then stopped and continued to stare at him. He walked towards her and stopped a few yards away. A conspiracy of silence seemed to reign between them, between us I should say, for by now I too was left simply staring, wondering what it was all about. It was he who finally broke the silence.

'Hi, Gladys. I hope I didn't surprise you too much?'

'How you find where I live?' Her voice was unusually restrained, though there was an ever so slight note of threat in it.

'Oh, I was jus' passing through the town. I ask at the Chinaman shop if they know you, an' they show me the way....'

After another long pause she beckoned to him to come inside. The door remained half-closed and I remained staring at it for the next fifteen minutes. Then I heard my mother calling me. My heart leapt at the thought of finally solving the mystery of the stranger. I found myself stuffing my shirt into my trousers respectfully. My mother called again, impatiently. I ran inside.

He was sitting on the only chair we had; she was on the edge of the bed. They both looked at me as I entered. I made sure to avoid his eyes, staring at her for refuge. Then after another long pause, she beckoned to him hesitantly and mumbled, 'Your father.'

I was a little surprised, of course, but not shocked. Perhaps more confused than anything else. I had known he existed somewhere in some shape. But my conception of him had been vague, formless. He had been part of my own personal folk-lore: something I had liked and at times dreamt about, like expensive gold-fish, but never really desired, never took quite seriously. Seeing him there before me, I was sure I would have been no less confounded had I been faced with Humpty-Dumpty. What could I say? What was I expected to say? They expected me to look at him. Well, I looked at him.

He had lines on his brow and his cheeks were rough. I thought he must shave every day; my friends had told me their fathers did. I thought it would have been very funny if my mother had had to shave every day too; I was not unconscious of my stupid notion.

He nodded in a gesture of approval as he stared at me.

'You are a fine boy' he said; and I wondered what he meant. Then he looked at my mother and in the same uncertain, unconvincing voice, he repeated, 'He's a fine boy.'

My mother murmured something in response, then glanced at me. Her eyes lacked the proud gleam of satisfaction which it usually bore when someone flattered me in this manner. Instead, it was slightly censorious: I could detect a hint of anger in them and I felt lost to explain why she should have reacted in this manner. When she looked away she held down her head, and if I hadn't known her so well I would have been convinced that there was shame in her eyes. After that she rested her elbow on her knee and her chin between her fingers and sighed, which I knew, was her silent, physical way of repeating an expression that was always on her lips: 'Oh, what a life, my God!'

I kept wondering what was going on. I had observed adults to act in the strangest way before; but underlying my ignorance, there had always been some gleam of understanding, some awareness, if ever so remote, that whatever they were up to was somehow meaningful. But the behaviour of my mother and the stranger now completely baffled me. Why didn't they say something? Did they hate each other? Did the fact that he was my father mean all that much to her?

Suddenly, I was overwhelmed with the fear that he had

come to take her away from me. Perhaps it was that which was worrying them. They did not know how to tell me. My mother would be leaving me all alone. In an instant, the essence of my relationship with her, the importance of her presence, impressed itself on me. I neither loved her nor hated her. I feared her a little, perhaps, for often she would beat me cruelly. But the rage I expressed then in my tears was purely an immediate reaction to the pain I felt. Somehow I conceived that beating me had meant far more to her than it had to me. The world was tough; so she often told me. I was her child and completely at her mercy; it was only natural. Despite everything, a strong bond held us together. Nothing positive, really; more the fear that if we lost each other we would have lost everything. For me she was the person I called mother: she gave me food, clothes and the books I read at school. And she taught me to be good. It was never quite clear what she meant by being good. More often than not, it simply meant *being good* to her, or not being ungrateful, which amounted to much the same thing. I suppose she could be said to have been warm in her own way. But unconsciously, she taught me not to expect very much and so I asked for very little. All I desired was for her to be there, always there. Now there was the threat of her departure.

But that was not possible. I reassured myself that I was being silly to the point of deciding that it would have been better if I left the room. Perhaps they wished to say adult things. As soon as I began to nudge my way to the door I heard him saying, in a manner which suggested that he was repeating himself, 'Yes, it's been a long time, Gladys.' I decided then that I was certainly the reason for their apparent discomfort, and I began to move less imperceptibly to the door. Suddenly I heard my mother call my name. Her voice was sharp and severe; she did not have to say that I must stay; her tone was enough.

The stranger looked at me quizzically, then back at her and suddenly sprang out of his chair. He made the usual motions which indicated an intention to depart; yet, he hesitated. Then he suddenly seemed to remember something. He took out a five-shilling note from his trouser pocket and handed it to me.

'Buy a present with it,' he said.

I stared at the note, a little shocked, both at the large sum of money and at the fact that he, of all people, should have given it to me. I looked up at my mother to see what her response was. I was not surprised when she said, 'Give it back.' Then she turned to him and said, 'I bring 'im up all this time without your help; I don't need it now.'

I immediately held the money out to him for I realized that my mother was in no mood to be crossed. I began to dread the moment when I would be alone with her.

The man began to protest, but he broke off suddenly and took back the note from me. I began to feel sorry for him, for he seemed insulted and sad. He took up his little felt hat, put it on his head and left without saying another word. I never saw him again.

A New Boy

V. S. Reid

*'A New Boy' by V. S. Reid, the distinguished Jamaican
novelist, is a story of the sea and the very special skill of
fishing from a small boat. But on another level, this ironical
fisherman's anecdote might be read as a timeless parable or
possibly a regional cautionary tale with a very definite uni-
versal ring of truth about it.*

The kingfish is a fighting fish with a turn of speed to blind
you. It slips up to the hook, long as your arm, shadow
boxing in the water. Sometimes it strikes like the wahoo,[1]
a nudge of the head and the bait is in his mouth. The jaws
are hung for strength and it can break the thread by a flip
of the backbone. The sea has groomed it sleekly, a racehorse
when the hook is in its mouth. He is unmatched, and it is
therefore agony to lose him.

Tina, the Jamaican girl, had given a fishing line to the
American, Kennedy, but for a long time, nothing happened.
And then a large one butted into his hook and took it for
thirty feet, tasting the sweet juices of the shrimp bait but
doing nothing else with it. He is sometimes a delicate eater.

At the noise from Kennedy, Ti Brooks, Tina's crewman,
came out of the bows and felt the line. Ti Brooks cried out
softly, incredulous at such good luck.

[1] *wahoo* – A large, swift deep-sea game fish, so named by the American
Indians.

'What is it, Ti?' Tina said.

'It's a dinner worthy of an archangel,' Ti Brooks said in a loud whisper.

The girl was at the rudder of the little fishing boat. She was glad the American had a fish on his line. The American tourists were strangers. Some came for half a year but went away strangers. They were neighbours whom one could hardly ever know, but a man with whom you fished from the same boat could not be hidden from you.

'Take your time, stranger,' Tina said.

'Fit for the high table in the Lodge! It's nothing less than a man-fish!' Ti Brooks cried again.

Tina shook her head violently at him. She could see the glint of tough humour in his eye. She knew the fishermen on the Jamaica north coast. She was one of them. This was her boat.

Ti Brooks touched the bellying line. His fingers wept with the desire to wrap themselves around such a link to good fortune. But a line engaged was inviolable.

Kennedy was not a fisherman. He was in the boat because he had been in the village and the girl had invited him to accompany them. He was a little ill at ease to find himself suddenly centre stage and he grinned weakly at the sea.

'Be kind to it,' Ti Brooks whispered in a fit of agitation. 'Treat it like a virgin. Do not punish it. It's a friendly fish. It contains the soul of my father who was a deacon, God rest the dead.'

'Shut up, you clown,' rasped Kennedy, sweaty with the fear of a suddenly slack line. The coil in the boat at his feet was thinning and he wanted to take in yardage. Tentatively, he yanked in a few inches.

'He has the hands of a cow. He's a banana boatman,'

G

groaned Ti Brooks, looking at Tina. 'The American is a *tush*.'[2]

'It's his fish, Ti Brooks,' Tina said sternly.

'The fish is for all of us. The profits will be shared as usual. This is a fishing boat, not a pretty plaything from one of the American hotels in Montego Bay,' said Ti Brooks.

Ti Brooks could not understand why God had driven up a kingfish from the deep and placed it on the American's hook, while his own hook was empty. He moved nearer to Kennedy.

The fish, twenty pounds of smart deepwater bone, muscle and ambrosial flesh, felt the line knead its flank and turned sharply right and then left again until the slack floated the line off its body. The line went dead in his hand and Kennedy covered his dismay with a small oath. Angrily, he commenced to recover the tackle but Ti Brooks cried out in pain:

'No, no! He's swimming back to us. He's our fish, he doesn't want you to lose him. Take the line in sweetly. Easy, as if you were with a virgin.'

Kennedy heard the rattle of the rudder posts and he turned to see the girl unshipping the heavy piece of wood, her wet arms shining in the sunlight. She took up the light-weight steering paddle and slipped it over the stern. Water whispered on the blade as she brought up the boat to meet the run of the fish. Kennedy wished she hadn't worn a skirt in the boat.

'Pay attention to the fish, man,' Tina said sharply. 'Has he swallowed the bait?'

[2] *tush* – A colloquial Jamaican expression to describe someone who is not up to much, an inept person, a poor fool; also a silly idea, an over-simple plan, nonsense.

The girl had sea sheen on her rounded arms and sleek dark face.

'How the devil do I know?' Kennedy said irritably.

'He'll call up the line and tell you,' Ti Brooks said gloomily, his elbows on the gunwale, hands cupping his face.

'He'll tug at the line. He'll be annoyed that the shrimp seems to have a tail too long for his throat,' Tina said.

'His lovely throat,' Ti Brooks said. He had forgotten his own line and was only deeply concerned with Kennedy's. 'I can see his throat down there now. Alone, his throat weighs five pounds. He's the best fish in the sea and the American has him on the hook.'

'Will you shut up?' Kennedy yelled.

'So now he'll frighten away the best fish in the sea. I think I should take the fish away from the American,' Ti Brooks said.

'You'll not touch that line. I command the boat,' Tina said.

'The boat is commanded by the fish that is on the hook,' Ti Brooks said.

'What's a fish? Maybe we'll leave him,' Tina said.

'Then haul him up and remove the hook from his mouth,' Ti Brooks grumbled.

For the American wants to fight him too early, Tina said to herself. He'll not wait for the fish to swallow the bait that he may have the bellyache. If I had my hand on the line, I'd play with him until he stood on his tail, begging me to stop, pleading with me to take him into the boat. With such a strong line, I'd play with him until he was weary and with no more fight left in him than in my toenail.

The low wooden boat rolled easily on the sea. The line jumped and ran through Kennedy's hand.

'He's swallowed the bait,' Tina said.

Kennedy tried the line and felt the fighting weight at the end.

'Now there're only two people in the world, you and the fish. But one of you will become a mule. The mule will die,' Ti Brooks said.

'What're you bleating about?' Kennedy said. He hoped they wouldn't notice the tremor in his fingers. He said to himself this wasn't sport, but heartbreak. He would play it cool. He looked sideways and he could see the pinks and blues of the hotels at Montego Bay.

'This is a good sized bite so near shore, isn't it?' he said to Tina, turning his head fully.

'Don't take your eye off the fish,' Tina warned.

'He's an expert. He can fish without looking, like riding no-hands,' Ti Brooks said instantly.

Kennedy turned to him and said, 'What the hell were you yakking about a mule?'

'If the fish becomes a mule and fights the line, then he'll tire and drown. If you become the mule and pull too hard on the line, then the line will break and you'll lose the fish.'

'How does that make me dead? That's what you said.'

'After he finds that he has broken the line, the fish will come back and eat you,' Ti Brooks explained.

Kennedy chuckled easily and turned back to the line. The sea had bright yellow and blue glints. He hoped the fish wouldn't do anything rash, like calling on him to show any real fishmanship. Up to now, it was almost like flying a kite. Except that inside, he sweated.

'Once upon a time I lost a fish and it came back for me,' Ti Brooks said, looking down into the water. 'I was a bow-

man that night and this was a swordfish. The swordfish put
his great big sword across the bows and said:
'"Stop the boat!"
'I said, "Why, Mr Swordfish?"
'He said, "The boat must be stopped for I've come back
for the man who lost me."
'So I said, "Do you know whose boat this is, Mr Swordfish?"
'And he gave a great roar of laughter and said, "What do
I care about whose boat this is? When I'm on the hook, I
command the boat. And I made a pledge down there that
if I got off the hook I'd return for the man who lost me for
my boat."
'So then, I said, "This boat belongs to an American
tourist."
'And the swordfish jumped and said, "What!" And he
took off as if a hundred tiger sharks were after him, for the
swordfish fear the tiger sharks. But do you know why he
fears the tourists?'
'No,' Kennedy said. 'Why?'
'Because the tourist would catch him and lose him again,
many times maybe, and he hates what the hook does to him
every time he's caught,' Ti Brooks said.
'Okay, lay off,' Kennedy said. He looked at Tina and
winked.
This one has a bit of bull heat in him, Tina said to herself.
But a man's made to prance. He's not much of a fisherman
either, but he hopes that by making a rocking chair out of
it, he'll fool us into believing he's good.
The fish leaped with a wet splash and at once Ti Brooks
swore that he recognized it. It was an old kingfish of his, an
infighter, liking to do battle on the surface.

'If you drag his head he'll go away and leave it on the hook. He's a fresh one,' warned Ti Brooks.

'Leave the man to fish,' Tina said.

Although he wasn't touching the line, Ti Brooks was working the fish equally with Kennedy. He signalled with cut and swoop of his hand, hunching down into the well of the boat whenever the fish dived, then tossing his head near enough to dislocate his neck when it executed in the air. He watched the wrist of the American as it hesitated over what to do when the fish threw itself about in the water and he chuckled over it. The foreigner was no fisherman.

'Do you know why the fish does that?' he asked Kennedy.

'He's showing off because he sees you watching him,' Kennedy joked tightly.

'He thinks that if he punishes himself by taking in air, he'll be purified of the strange sickness in his belly. We fishermen say he's taking medicine,' Ti Brooks explained.

'The man's fighting him well,' Tina said.

'Ah, leave me alone, let me help the American,' Ti Brooks said disgustedly. Here was a chance to reap some fun from one of the white bodied foreigners who lay out in the sun making butcher stalls of the beaches a man had so freely used one time.

Tina knew when the fish weakened for now it took less to the air. Kennedy sensed the movement in Ti Brooks and he caught a glimpse of the gaff in the fisherman's hand. He growled at Ti Brooks that he'd do all there was to be done. He wanted no help with it.

The fish had narrowed its field of inquiry. It now fought sluggishly, resting a little more on the hook that had been placed there to destroy it. Tina knew the details of the drama being enacted under the sea's skin. She was not sad for the fish. It was the man who was on the hook. He had the look of triumph. A small wave curled and flung spray on her face. She pushed down on the paddle and brought the boat around, presenting a beam for Kennedy to bring in his fish. The big head was rearing out of the water, fighting the hook like a rebellious pony. The powerful backbone curved and it smashed down. Kennedy's hands commenced swallowing the line in great gulps. The ache at his wrists was sweet.

'No,' Tina said softly.

'No!' Ti Brooks bellowed.

But Kennedy's hands were gathering in the line in a glad rush. He laid his grasping hands into it, his lips parted, a keen rejoicing in his head. Ti Brooks made a snatch at the line and Kennedy shouldered him off and jerked hard.

The line parted.

Ti Brooks left the boat like a bolt and struck the water with his hands blindly reaching. The tides swung the line and Ti Brooks missed.

Ti Brooks climbed back into the boat and sat with his head bowed. Spume touched her face again and Tina untied the sail furled on the bamboo boom. She would catch a small wind to go in on.

'I'll pay for the fish that got away,' Kennedy said.

Ti Brooks went forward and raised the sail. He stood there holding on to the bamboo mast and watched the dead fish float past. Tina looked too and looked away. Kennedy saw it.

'I'll pay for the fish that got away,' Kennedy said.

The sail caught the wind and the boat kicked. They passed the dead fish and the sea was empty.

'It was my fish. I'm the loser,' Kennedy said angrily.

'The boat's the loser,' Tina said.

'That's not what you said before,' Kennedy said.

'The fish was yours when you had him on the hook. You had it in your power to make us a little richer. But now that you've lost him, it's the boat's loss,' the girl said.

They sailed on and soon they could hear the gusty laughter of the American tourists on the hotel beaches of Montego Bay.

'I'm not a fisherman,' Kennedy said.

'You were a tourist before, but once you had the line in your hand, you became a fisherman,' Tina said. 'This is a fishing boat.'

Kennedy looked at the girl aft and he could see most of her nubile beauty. He wished she hadn't worn a skirt in the boat.

'I'll hire your boat tomorrow. I want to learn to fish.'

Tina thought that she would hire him the boat for it was no use being angry. A man had to learn to fish, like sawing wood or making shoes or fixing engines, whatever. But she was glad he hadn't enquired why they hadn't recovered the dead fish. At least he'd known that the fish must come into the boat alive. He'd be a fisherman, one day.

A Death

Mervyn Morris

'A Death' is an extremely moving account of a Jamaican schoolboy's first glimpse of the hypocrisy of grief in the adult world. Its author, Mervyn Morris, a Jamaican school-master and a well-known poet, has written a harsh and realistic story which will 'connect' with all its young readers and, more personally, with those who have themselves had a death in their family.

'Wake up! Wake up, Trevor!'

The voice spoke again, quietly as before, calmly insistent.

'Wake up, Trevor! Wake up!'

Trevor turned over and tried to look up. At first, he could see nothing; it was quite dark. In a moment, he became more fully aware of a hulking shape leaning over him. The voice spoke again.

'Wake up, Trevor, wake up!'

'Yes?' said Trevor.

'Come, you've got to go home.'

'Go home?'

'Yes, go home. Your Daddy's very sick.'

'Sick? Daddy?'

Trevor recognized the voice at last; it was Uncle Arthur's. He swung out of bed and called for a light.

A bright flashlight was put to lie on its side on top of one of the open lockers the boys put their clothes in. By its light, Trevor put on his school khaki and, as his uncle

105

suggested, packed some other clothes in a small grip he kept under his bed.

'Bring your blue suit,' Uncle Arthur said.

'What's the time?'

His uncle stuck his wrist into the light.

'Twenty past two.'

The small party left quietly, more or less quietly, for three of them trod on the loose floorboard just outside the dormitory door. Jones, the night watchman, lighted their way down the wooden steps on to the stone steps and under the heavy stone arches.

It was very windy outside and cold. Trevor buttoned his blazer and shuddered. They made their way over to the Head's house where a lamp was burning. The Head, in his dressing gown, weary but trying to look hospitable, offered a cup of coffee. Trevor's uncle refused politely, and the party of three climbed into the car in the Headmaster's driveway. As they drove off, the headlights flashed into view the chapel front and the cross on the solitary grave outside.

'Do you pray?' Trevor's uncle asked.

'Yes.'

'Then pray. Your father's very sick.'

'Is he dying?'

'Yes.'

When they arrived home, the sky was lightening. Trevor was told to go to bed. He searched the house for his mother, but she was at the hospital.

The tension of the next three days was not exactly hard to bear. Trevor felt it should have been, but he knew that what he felt was neither tension nor grief; it was a curious emptiness, a strange suspension of feeling, as though they were all waiting for something to happen which might make them really feel the gravity of the occasion more personally.

Travelling to and from the hospital with his mother, Trevor had a sense of not belonging to the whole drama. He knew it was a drama. His mother was distraught and grief-stricken, uneasily silent, and she had a way of hugging him suddenly in those few hours they spent at home. He could see his father was dying. His father could recognize no one, not even Trevor's mother. He just lay there on his back, most of the time with his eyes closed, breathing noisily through his mouth, his hands limply on the bed. Trevor's mother sat on a hard chair gazing at her husband, sometimes intently, sometimes blankly as though she was thinking of something else.

Finally, on Wednesday afternoon, at about four o'clock, the sick man seemed to snatch his breath. His wife sat up with a jerk; she was rigid.

'Nurse! Nurse!' She paused. 'Go and call the nurse.' She sent Trevor.

When his father actually stopped breathing, Trevor was not so much disturbed as interested in a detached way. His father's breathing simply stopped. His whole body and especially his face seemed not so much to slump as, at first, to relax peacefully. Then, in a moment, his face became expressionless. A nurse slipped in his dentures and pulled the sheet over his head.

Trevor's mother was sobbing. She got up from her chair, put her hands to her face and, standing quite erect, cried quietly. When she took her hands away at last and turned to look at her husband again, there was a curtain around the bed. She caught sight of Trevor. The tears started again, quite silently this time. To Trevor they seemed like tired tears, tears almost of relief.

None of his uncles being there at the critical time, Trevor and his mother approached a waiting taxi. As they neared it they were met by the Reverend Thomas, the rector.

'Good evening, Mrs Franklin,' he said, and smiled cheeringly. 'How are you?'

'Not too bad, thank you,' she mumbled.

'And how's your husband today?'

She began to cry again.

'He's dead, Rector.'

Wordless, the rector grasped her hand. He helped her into the taxi and watched it leave.

In a short time they were at home. The news had been broken and the condoling friends had begun to appear. A sister-in-law slipped a sedative into the warm milk she handed to Trevor's mother, and later put her to bed.

The uncles appeared shortly, and Trevor watched and listened to them make the necessary arrangements. They arranged the radio announcement, the press notice, the minister, the grave-space, and the time of the funeral.

Trevor watched the compulsive mourners arrive later, the ones who talked about the last time they saw his father and what a fine man he was. Trevor knew that he was too young to judge anybody, but he knew that they were all frauds. Their display of grief followed a prearranged pattern, as though they had been practising. Trevor watched them and felt like being rude.

The funeral took place the following day. More harrowing than the funeral was the preparation that led up to it. All morning, Trevor's aunts were busy preparing sandwiches and wrapping them in napkins or in grease-paper to keep them fresh. At about two o'clock the body arrived. Trevor's mother undid the wooden slab that covered the oval porthole through which his father's face could be seen. The face looked unnatural; it looked, in fact, prepared. Trevor's mother kept going away from the body and coming back to look plaintively at the dead overwashed face. Eventually she was persuaded to retire to her room and get dressed for the funeral. By three-thirty, she was at the front door and ready to meet her friends with stoic pride.

One by one, having expressed their formal or warm condolences, depending on their sense of fitness, they filed past the coffin and peered through the glass at the dead face of Trevor's father. The sillier ones said, 'Gawn to rest, Amen!' and Trevor suppressed his amusement. All around the front of the house were groups of people, he discovered, competing with each other to decide who had known the dead man the most personally and who had seen him last. Trevor tried his best to look like a child of grief and not to seem angry at all the middle-aged people who had called him 'little man'.

The rector arrived just before four o'clock. Standing with his back to the black piano, he prayed briefly. The coffin was lifted from the chairs in the drawing room and placed into the hearse. Trevor was bundled with his mother into the chauffeur-driven car of a rich man whom he did not know; in fact the man had been a churchwarden with his father. Trevor did not mind: the Studebaker was comfortable.

At the church Trevor's mother clutched her son's hand tightly. Trevor noticed that under her black veil she appeared to be crying, but she held her body with erect dignity and she did not wipe her eyes.

'God moves in a mysterious way
His wonders to perform ...'

The words made Trevor angry. Who was God, he wondered, and why could nobody understand Him? He
thought of chapel sermons at school, of the unsolved
puzzles, the unanswered questions they had raised.

Those other hymns, he thought, seemed far more suitable. Of course, he could not help wondering how many
people understood the peculiar construction of the line,
'Praise my soul, the King of Heaven'. How many people
didn't bother to think at all? How many thought the soul
was King of Heaven? *'Abide With Me'* he could remember
hearing his father play, and often, the harmonies he impro-
vized so sure and so complex.

*'And though after my skin worms destroy this body, yet
in my flesh shall I see God ...'* What did that mean?

The eulogy struck Trevor as sincere. The rector seemed
really to know his father. Trevor was surprised. He had
thought it would be empty piety, but it was not. He felt
like crying for the first time that day. Looking through
misty eyes beyond the rector where he stood in the aisle,
he could see the brass cross on the altar, just like the wooden
one at school. He could remember too that only a year ago
his father had still been singing in the choir, standing near
the cross which was held at the head of the choir procession.

When the church service was over, the large congregation
walked down the main aisle and out towards the grave.

The procession followed the pall-bearers down to the
burial spot which was under a tree. Would the tree give
shade or would the dead leaves drop on the grave and keep
it dirty? Did it matter?

The spadework at the sides of the grave was so smooth that the hole seemed to sparkle in parts. There were a lot of wreaths on the ground.

The coffin was put on the straps across the grave. Trevor looked around at the other spectators. They looked uniformly sad.

'Man that is born of woman hath but a short time to live, and is full of misery. He cometh up, and is cut down, like a flower; he fleeth as it were a rainbow, and never continueth in one stay.

'In the midst of life we are in death ...'

His mother tightened her grip on his hand.

The creak of the rollers was obscene, even more so than the first thud of dirt on the coffin. His mother began to cry.

To Trevor it was fantastic to observe the change that seemed to come over the gathering within moments of the last pat on the mound of the grave. He watched the wreath-bearers step forward proudly to lay their wreaths.

And then, quite suddenly, the conversations began; the smiles appeared on their faces, and the atmosphere of the funeral was such that it might have been a garden party. Even Trevor's mother seemed to be trying to fit in with the new mood, baring her teeth bravely in a faint smile, if without conviction.

'Well, little man, you must take care of your mother.'

Trevor nodded.

'Now, you are the man of the family, son.'

Trevor looked solemn and responsible. How much do people understand? he thought. What is grief? What is condolence for?

'Well, son, what I always say is "In the midst of death

we are in life".' The man laughed. 'Cheer up now and try and forget the past!'

What am I to say when I get back to school? Trevor wondered. I'll be the centre of attraction for a while. How should I behave? What do people want? What will they expect of me?

'Well, young man,' he heard one of his uncles say, 'we're proud of you. I didn't see you cry.'

Trevor's mother tightened her hold on his hand. And Trevor smiled sadly.

A House in Another Country

Neville Dawes

This extract is taken from The Last Enchantment, *the first novel by the Jamaican poet and novelist, Neville Dawes. The editor is responsible for the extract and its title. The story is about one of the eccentric influences of English university education on a certain kind of 'returned' graduate during the colonial period in Jamaica; it also illustrates the near-farcical syndrome of 'shade, class and inferiority' in the West Indian* bourgeoisie.

The Phillips' house had originally been a plantation Great House. It was hidden away and difficult to find, for though it was only four miles from Half Way Tree, it was 'in the country', and, in a sense, in another country. You half expected, while walking up the circular drive, to see massive bloodhounds bound at you and to see footmen in livery and carriages and house-slaves and plantation-slaves in white calico near the white-washed outhouses.

Ramsay Tull turned in from the endless marl road and walked up the tarred drive. The place was deep in poinciana and the rose garden, brilliantly in bloom in the centre of the front lawn, was stylized and artificial and in the very best taste. He saw the stables on his left and the fine horses he didn't know were fine because horses were things you rode in the country if you couldn't afford a car. And there was the incongruous car (instead of a carriage) parked by the steps to the front veranda: a shiny new Buick Roadmaster,

jet-black and trimmed with silver. He walked by and
smelled the upholstery, sickly-sweet like the seats at the
Carib Theatre.[1] The smell of new cars was one he had not
been born to and he disliked it because it reminded him of
asafoetida and feet with yaws. He glimpsed, on the lawn at
the side of the house, a high thin badminton net.

It was four-fifteen in the afternoon, oppressive and
thundery with one of those tropical mirages where the hills
and the clouds seem to be on top of you because they have
shielded the sun. The veranda was a post-slavery addition
but seemed to have the browning of age hidden by the
deliberate creeper which he thought was honeysuckle. The
house seemed specially well kept, as if a house was not a
place for a man to live in but an adornment to be gathered
round him. It seemed incredible to Ramsay that in tiny
Jamaica there could be another distinct world of graceful
dwellings. He felt he might be entering an afternoon in
Henry James's *Portrait of a Lady*,[2] and Mrs Phillips would
have been delighted to hear of this feeling because her home
was planned to trap the visitor into literature.

The male voice he heard in the drawing room, however,
was definitely Jamaican. It echoed a little because the room
was deep and panelled. Ramsay knocked and somewhere in
the gloom Mrs Phillips said, 'Come in, Mr Tull. Did you
find your way?'

She was sitting on the largest sofa Ramsay had ever seen,
smothered in cushions, and a young man sat on a low chair

[1] *Carib Theatre* – A Jamaican cinema. One of the largest in the West
Indies.

[2] *Portrait of a Lady* – A novel by Henry James (1843-1916), the American writer. *Portrait of a Lady* is one of James's early works, in which he
presents various types of Americans transplanted into a European environ-
ment.

near the piano. He didn't stop talking when Mrs Phillips greeted Ramsay. He was one of Mrs Phillips' poets, a fair-complexioned man with straight hair. His face was round and quizzical with the eyes sunk far in as in a mask. You remembered his slow, perpetual and slightly sardonic smile, his flat, broad Jamaican accent (which was out of keeping with his hair) and the impression he gave of not listening to what other people said in conversation. His name was Stephen Strachan and he wrote good nationalist verse in the very manner of Walt Whitman and unconvincing love poetry which read like an inaccurate translation of Latin poetry into Elizabethan English. Mrs Phillips had discovered and made him.

'You think, Madonna, I could ever agree to that?' Stephen Strachan was saying when Ramsay sat on the edge of the sofa where Mrs Phillips had patted him an invitation. All the artists and writers under her wing and all the People's Democratic followers and all her servants called Mrs Phillips 'Madonna'. 'So, I told him the whole bureaucratic structure stinks with unimaginative pen-pushers like him.'

Mrs Phillips said, 'What I like about you, Stephen, is you've got guts!'

Well, she was almost an artist, anyway, and you could see that clearly all over the room. From where he sat Ramsay was looking at a painting of a scene of fishermen catching crabs. To the left of the painting was an enormous box with the loudspeaker extension from the radiogram, but his eyes wandered back to the painting. If you didn't know much about painting you saw three stooping figures, three irregular splashings not as dark as the background which wasn't trees or mountains but a flat ungraded blackness and the light in the picture came from a moon that threw no shadows but silvered the sea-foam in the foreground. It reminded Ramsay of a beach in the parish of St Ann. 'I must start learning how to talk about painting.' he thought.

Stephen Strachan told how he abused the civil servant but Ramsay hadn't heard what the civil servant had done.

'Do you write?' Mrs Phillips asked Ramsay abruptly.

He was slow in adjusting to the question for he found himself thinking that the question meant 'Can you write?' Then he thought of lying and finally said, 'No.'

'I've got an itch to write a poem,' Stephen Strachan said, 'but I want a subject.'

'Isn't the actual writing more like the end of a kind of apathy out of which you have to drive yourself, Keats' feeling of lassitude?' Mrs Phillips asked, thinking her way seriously to the heart of the problem. 'Don't you think so, Mr Tull?'

Mrs Phillips was not being perverse; she was only being a colonial educated abroad. The situation is that the colonial goes to Britain or America or Europe and copies the attitudes and vocabulary of a certain period then returns to a static society and lives, from then on, in the flavour of an era that Britain or America or Europe has forgotten. A day's fashion becomes permanent and lasts for a lifetime. Mrs Phillips had been in England in the 'twenties. She always began her 'influences' by trying to shock the neophyte into a new type of reality, a one-woman crusade against the entrenched puritan conscience of the Jamaican. But Ramsay had grown up in a tougher world.

'Write a poem about the new Buick which the People's Democratic Party has bought,' Mrs Phillips commissioned.

'The modern machine, in what is really a primitive political situation.'

'I could try it,' Stephen said, with the sardonic smile of the poet. 'What I like about the car is the way the black sets off the silver.'

'Something symbolic probably,' she said, gently feeding him the idea. 'But you haven't had any tea, Mr Tull. Ramsay, isn't it? We are having coffee, actually, you know, like 'coffee-tea' in the country.' She got up and poured the coffee from a long silver pot and did it gracefully and smiled down at him when she handed him the cup. She pushed a trolley with two plates of sliced chocolate cake in front of him.

'Madonna, I must go,' Stephen said.

'Stephen is going to spend a week at Cinchona,' she told Ramsay, to bring him into the conversation.

They were all three standing with the awkwardness that sometimes follows abrupt decisions to depart. The situation needed a phrase and Mrs Phillips found it. She said, like a benediction, 'The hills. I think the hills will perform their usual magic, Stephen.'

She went into the study adjoining the drawing room, and Stephen studied the Picasso above the piano.

Then she returned and said, 'I shan't be a minute, Ramsay, I'm going to take Stephen to Constant Spring Road.'

The Buick glided away.

Ramsay walked around the room looking at things, the radiogram that was about five feet long, the Bechstein,[3] the single row of new books on a low built-in shelf beside the radiogram. Then he peeped into the study which had more

[3] *Bechstein* – A celebrated make of piano.

books and bookshelves than the Surrey College library. On top of one shelf was a framed photograph of Mrs Phillips's husband, Dr Phillips, in army uniform.

Then Ramsay heard a car enter the drive and he hurried back to the sofa.

It was not Mrs Phillips but her daughter Patricia. She was dressed for tennis: white shorts and a white long-sleeved jumper. Patricia was handsome and athletic-looking like her father and she had a cool sandalwood complexion. She had been at school in England all during the war and it was only a few months since she had returned to Jamaica. She was nearly eighteen and was doing her last school year at St Andrew's High School for girls. Ramsay was seeing her for the first time.

'Hullo!' she said. 'Nobody home?' She didn't only sound English; she *was* an English girl.

'Mrs Phillips jus' went out,' Ramsay said, and heard his own very flat voice.

She stood over the trolley. 'Choc'late cake! Do you mind if I have my tea? I'm famished!' She sat beside him. 'Are you a painter?'

'No, I'm jus' here.'

'No, don't tell me. Let me guess. You are a writer!'

'No. I'm Ramsay—'

'Oh, I *know*. You're in politics. No? I give up. Won't you have some coffee?'

He didn't reply till she poured herself a cup of coffee, put milk and sugar in it and sat down again. It suddenly seemed to him that what he had to say was extremely important.

'I'm Ramsay Tull,' he said. 'I'm going to England next week and Mrs Phillips invited me to tea.'

'Oh, *you're* the scholarship winner. Aren't you lucky!'

The trouble about a quick English accent, Ramsay realized, is that you can listen to it but you can't talk to it.

'I think this choc'late cake's delicious, don't you?'

The 'don't you' irritated him. He thought of Arnold Bennett's *The Card*[4] and decided to be 'innocent'. She was only a Jamaican girl, for her skin said so.

'Why you talk like that?' he asked her.

She laughed, throwing her head back. 'Oh, I don't know. I just *talk* like that, I suppose.'

'Is your car outside there?'

'No, it's really Mummy's car, you know, but she's using the Buick today. D'you know, a *stupid* policeman stopped me this afternoon and wanted to see my driver's licence. Why are Jamaican policemen so *stupid!* I told him it was at home and anyway I had twenty-four hours in which to produce it. He didn't know *that*, of course. But I've got to be more careful, Daddy'll be furious.'

'How you like St Andrew's?'

'Oh, I *hate* it,' she said. 'D'you know, I don't like Jamaica at all. Except the weather, of course. The weather's gorgeous! Anyway I'll only be here until I'm ready to go to Cambridge. I'm going to Girton,[5] you know, where Mummy was. Where are you going?'

'I'm not sure,' Ramsay said.

She stood up and smiled at him in the English way, the lips slightly puckered and the eyes wide open. It struck him that you could learn even a way of smiling from another race.

---

[4] *The Card* – A farcical novel about the interaction of innocence and experience, written by Arnold Bennett (1867-1931), the English novelist.

[5] *Girton* – A Cambridge University college for women.

She walked across the room and switched on a tall green-shaded standard lamp. She posed, just for a few seconds, beside the lamp and then went upstairs.

When Mrs Phillips returned, Ramsay's first impulse was to go before it became dark. He needed to go now because he did not want to spend the time wishing that she would take him to Constant Spring Road in the Buick. He was uncomfortable because he was afraid that Dr Phillips might come in at any moment and also he thought he heard preparations for dinner somewhere in the background.

Mrs Phillips shifted a lounge chair and sat facing him with her back to the lamp. She talked to him about Stephen Strachan and, in the green light, he felt he was being drawn into a conspiracy. She thought that Stephen had read too much, hadn't assimilated it all and that he ought to write prose because his poetry tended to be lumpy and clogged. The odd thing about Stephen, she said, was that he didn't seem to have any proper 'inspiration' of his own. He only wrote things *she* asked him to write for she only had to say, 'Come, Stephen, write me a poem about this or that' and he would write some of his best stuff. She wanted to know if Ramsay thought this was odd.

He was preparing himself to say it was time to go when she started talking again.

'The real danger about our artistic awakening is that it's too closely linked to a political awakening. I am afraid that when the political enthusiasm dies, the artists will either have to start all over again, or die, too. It isn't that they can't observe or are writing political tracts. They have feeling all right, but it's political feeling. Don't you follow?'

'But they will have important historical value,' Ramsay

said. It was an adequate phrase which avoided judgment.

'Of course, they will have, as you suggest, important historical value.' Ramsay was flattered, as she intended he should be, because she had repeated the phrase he used. 'But what is going to happen to them personally? The artist, surely, is something like a medium with a seance table; the mediocre artist borrows somebody else's table but the great artist builds his own. Stephen has no personal seance table, if you see what I mean. Take away the progressive movement which is going on in this country at the moment, so that we hear only the Walt Whitman[6] phraseology and not the new urgent Jamaican voice that is striking a new chord today ...' She let that hover for a while. 'The painters and sculptors are all right; they can go on for years on technique alone till they have a new experience that will require a significant modification of the technique. But poor Stephen doesn't have the technique. He's only got words, I'm afraid, and he is so sensitive that you can't talk to him about it.'

Two things irritated Ramsay. One was that Mrs Phillips did not talk about his going to England, and the other was that he didn't know just how to go about leaving Mrs Phillips. He remembered reading recently in one of Dr Joad's[7] books that at Oxford and Cambridge you learn how to enter a room and how to leave it.

'You never say anything,' she laughed. 'I have no idea what you are thinking. Perhaps you should write. Why don't you write? You never know. We have things stored in odd corners of our minds.'

---

[6] *Walt Whitman* – The American poet (1819-1892), famous for his *Leaves of Grass*, a sequence of twelve poems which, in his own words, is saturated 'with the vehemence of pride and audacity of freedom ...'

[7] *Dr Joad* – Dr C. E. M. Joad, the English philosophical writer.

Why had she invited him to tea? He had come prepared to talk about himself, about going to England.

'It's very easy to forget Jamaica when you go away,' she said. 'Have you met Patricia?'

'Yes.'

'After eight years in England she simply can't adjust.'

This, Ramsay thought, was the time to go, and he moved to the edge of the sofa.

He managed to get up and she said, 'Do you have to go?'

On the veranda, he saw the flowing lines of the long Buick and the smaller Morris Minor near the stables.

'I think you will be a writer, Ramsay. Oxford will bring that out. Only don't get mixed up in left-wing politics, please. The writer has to keep himself clean. The war against Germany hasn't at all deceived me about the true nature of Communism. But you *will* write. I mean, you may become a *writer*. Good-bye, Ramsay, and good luck. Don't forget Jamaica!'

He felt, as they shook hands, that he had always known her. He walked the mile and a half back to the Constant Spring Road. He had the feeling that he had spent the afternoon in England.

Biographical Notes

C. L. R. JAMES. Trinidad (1901). Educated at Queen's Royal College, Trinidad. Journalist, broadcaster, West Indian political analyst, and an acknowledged commentator on Shakespeare's *Tragedies*. Has written many books.

SAMUEL SELVON. Trinidad (1923). Educated in Trinidad. Journalist, broadcaster, and the winner of three literary Fellowships. Lives in London. Has written several books.

MICHAEL ANTHONY. Trinidad (1932). Educated at Mayaro Roman Catholic School and the Junior Technical School, San Fernando, Trinidad. Works at Reuters in London. Has written several novels.

CLIFFORD SEALY. Trinidad (1927). Educated in Trinidad and at St Luke's College, Exeter, Devon. Former free lance radio journalist with the B B C. One of the first contributors to the BBC's literary programme 'Caribbean Voices'. After many years in London, he returned to Port of Spain where he now edits *Voices*, a West Indian literary quarterly and manages The Book Shop in Marli Street. His poems, stories and plays have been published in the West Indies, and his latest play, *The Professor* has been published in the Caribbean Plays Series.

GEORGE LAMMING. Barbados (1927). Educated in Barbados. Broadcaster, lecturer, novelist and an outstanding poetry-reader. Lives in London. Has been awarded three distinguished literary Fellowships.

EDWARD BRATHWAITE. Barbados (1930). Educated in Barbados and at Pembroke College, Cambridge University. Lecturer in History at the University of the West Indies. Has written poetry, plays and short stories which have been broadcast on the B B C and published in Britain and the West Indies.

JAN CAREW. Guyana (1922). Educated at Berbice High School, Guyana, Howard University, America, and Prague University. Has lived in many European countries and in Russia. Now lives in Guyana. Has had four plays produced on British television, many poems and short stories published in Britain, America and the West Indies, and has written several books.

EDGAR MITTELHOLZER. Guyana (1909). Was educated at Berbice High School, Guyana, and privately afterwards. Was awarded a Guggenheim Fellowship (the first awarded to a West Indian writer) for his *Kaywana* trilogy which he offered as his 'project' for the Fellowship. Lived in England for seventeen years where he died tragically in 1965. Wrote twenty-five books.

JOHN HEARNE. Jamaica (Born in Canada, 1926). Educated at Jamaica College, Edinburgh University, and London University. Served in the Royal Air Force. Taught in an English Grammar school and in other schools in London.

Now lives in Jamaica where he has also taught in secondary schools. At present on the staff of the Extra-Mural Department in the University of the West Indies. Regular contributor of pseudonymous articles in the *Sunday Gleaner* and has written *Our Heritage* with Rex Nettleford and several novels. Hearne was awarded the distinguished John Llewellyn Rhys Memorial Prize in London.

H. ORLANDO PATTERSON. Jamaica (1940). Educated at Kingston College, Jamaica, University College of the West Indies and London School of Economics where he is now an assistant lecturer in Sociology. He wrote his Ph.D. thesis on the Social Psychology of Slavery. Has contributed to many literary and political reviews in London, and has written several novels.

V. S. REID. Jamaica (1913). Educated in Jamaica. A leading journalist, magazine editor, founder-member of the Jamaica Press Association, novelist, and winner of two literary Fellowships. Has always lived in Jamaica and was the first West Indian novelist to contribute a book to the Blue Mountain Library Series for young readers.

MERVYN MORRIS. Jamaica (1937). Educated at Munro College, Jamaica, University College of the West Indies, and at St Edmund Hall, Oxford University. Rhodes Scholar, lawn-tennis 'Blue' in 1959-60 and 1961, and the winner of the Institute of Race Relations Essay Competition, established in 1963, with *Feeling, Affection, Respect*. Has had his radio essays and poems broadcast on the B B C and published in the West Indies. At present Senior English Master at his old school, Munro College, where he is working on his first book of poems. Has had three poems included in *Young Commonwealth Poets '65*, a publication sponsored by the Commonwealth Festival of Arts, 1965.

NEVILLE DAWES. Born (1926) in Nigeria of Jamaican parents. Educated at Jamaica College and Oriel College, Oxford University. Visiting Professor of English at the University of Guyana (1963-4), and now Senior Lecturer in English at the University of Ghana. Poems and short stories broadcast on the B B C and published in West Indian magazines and literary reviews. Has so far written two novels.

Acknowledgments

The Editor and Publishers are grateful to the authors for permission to include their work in this Anthology. They are also indebted to Mrs. Jacqueline Mittelholzer for permission to include *Tacama* by her late husband, Edgar Mittelholzer; to Faber & Faber Ltd. for *The Hurricane* from 'The Faces of Love' by John Hearne; to 'Bim', Volume 3, No. 12 for *As Time Goes By* by Samuel Selvon; and to 'Focus 1960', an anthology of contemporary Jamaican writing, edited by Edna Manley, for *A New Boy* by V. S. Reid.